BY WAY OF WYOMING

Over a rugged pass that shut off Shadrock, Wyoming, from the rest of the world, came Brad Hunter driving his "Tall T" trail herd, crisply explaining to the curious that he was pushing his herd to Ellsworth, Kansas, by way of Wyoming.

The Texans who had followed him up the trail waited impatiently for him to take up the feud that had hung over him like a dark cloud. He did not seem to be in a hurry. He waited until others moved, until grim Newt Norton took the warpath, until Ed Martin was in full flight, until the Sloping S ranch had disintegrated. Then he stepped in to take a leading hand, only to find that the hate he carried in his heart was never his own, and that the trail of life, for him, led back to Texas.

BY WAY OF WYOMING

Curtis Bishop

GUNSMOKE

This hardback edition 2008
by BBC Audiobooks Ltd
by arrangement with
Golden West Literary Agency

ISBN 978 1 405 68224 4

British Library Cataloguing in Publication Data available.

Printed and bound in Great Britain by
CPI Antony Rowe, Chippenham, Wiltshire

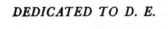

DEDICATED TO D. E.

BY WAY OF WYOMING

Chapter One

THE TRAIL HERD came over the pitch and roll of Sunrise Pass into the lush flats where Frenchman's Creek joined the Dry Devil's River—which belied its name in this gentle Wyoming summer with a thin muddy stream that was hock-high in the bends.

And there, as the gaunt trail-weary longhorns scented water and broke into a dead run, the Tall T outfit from Texas met its first challenge from Wyoming men.

It was inevitable that this challenge finally come. This was a dead-end valley in northern Wyoming, many miles off the trail route of any cattlemen except the three ranchmen who ran stock in its flatlands; and their herds always pushed across the divide going east, never west. Never before had a trail herd come into this valley from any direction, much less as far south and west as Texas; and across the river Jupiter Cross and Sledge Mahoney were as curious and as antagonistic as Ed Martin, whose Sloping S range the Texas cattle were now running over, and who was waiting at the trail fork with a half-dozen riders, each one grimly challenging.

Ed Martin was a broad-shouldered man, and his face was coated with a short thick stubble which made him seem darker, both in complexion and in mood. Even if it had not been his range, probably Martin would have made the first challenge to a stranger, while Sledge Mahoney and Jupiter Cross waited peacefully if impatiently. He had the look of a man who could foresee an issue, and who would ride straight out to meet it. Not bull-like, not insanely. He was also a man who could be clever, and would certainly weigh the probabilities and the odds; but he would not be afraid— not even of a larger outfit than this mysterious Tall T crew, which was big enough with its three trail wagons and its score of riders, all armed and good riding men from the way they sat their horses and moved their stock.

A lean red-haired man also took in this newly come spread with appraising eyes, and then kneed his pony closer to Martin as two men left the trail herd and rode slowly to where Ed Martin and his Sloping S cowboys waited impatiently, but motionlessly; this was Cherry Carr, the Sloping S riding boss, whose grin was as dangerous as Ed Martin's darkness. The other Sloping S riders followed the foreman's example and went limp in their saddles, relaxing against the moment that might see them in swift deadly action.

And all watched the two Texas men come on with the same look—narrow, appraising, hostile.

"By God!" Cherry whispered to his boss. "They ain't packing hardware!"

Ed Martin nodded. He had also noticed this with a sharp curiosity that had registered other bits of information: that the Texas men were young, and that they rode good horses. There were rifles in well oiled scabbards; but when men ride close, and talk almost stirrup to stirrup, a rifle is a useless thing. He scowled, and his challenging voice rang out before the Texans had closed the space between them.

"This is Sloping S country. Get your cattle off my land, and be damned quick about it."

There was no answer, not then. The first responding speech was from the younger of the two strangers. The

2

dust of several states stained his hat and boots, and his shirt was tattered and soiled; but his air was that of a man used to giving orders, and having them obeyed. His eyes met Martin's sullen glare, and Cherry Carr, pushing even closer to his boss, saw their twinkle, as if there was a joke about all this which nobody but Texas men would ever appreciate.

"Howdy, gents," the stranger drawled. "Mite hot today, ain't it? Even for July."

"We got no time for visiting," Martin said curtly. "Get your ramrod up here. This is my grass, and I ain't lending it or selling it."

"Reckon I'm the ramrod, friend," was the polite answer. "This is the Tall T outfit from Texas. I'm the owner, Brad Hunter. This is Squint Elliott, my foreman."

"Howdy, gents," the second Texan said in the same exaggerated mildness—one glance at his wrinkled face revealed how he had received his nickname. He rolled a cigarette calmly, one leg thrown over the neck of his sleek roan mare. From all appearances he regarded this meeting as nothing more than an opportunity to pass the time of day with future friends.

"I'm Ed Martin of the Sloping S," snapped the dark-bearded man. "Get out of here by sundown if you don't want trouble."

The man called Brad Hunter took off his hat and wiped his perspiring face with a soiled kerchief. Sun tan was deeper on his face than on the Sloping S riders, telling its story of longer and hotter days, and of raw wind on his cheeks. "That's plumb peculiar," he murmured. "I was told down in Texas that the mouth of Frenchman's Creek was open range. Mebbe we got our wires crossed and come to the wrong place."

3

"This is Frenchman's Creek," Martin snarled, "but it plays hell being open range. What are you doing in Sunset Valley anyhow? There ain't a market within five hundred miles and no open range any closer than the badlands."

"Just moseying through the country," grinned the Texan. "Heard plenty of talk about it. Bragging talk. Was driving to market anyhow and thought we might as well come this way."

Martin's eyes widened. The Texan was talking like a fool. But Brad Hunter's grin showed that he knew how silly it sounded, and was amused at Martin's amazement.

"From Texas!" snorted the Sloping S owner. "You drive a herd from Texas to Kansas by way of Wyoming!"

Brad Hunter nodded. "Does seem out of the way," he admitted.

Squint Elliott, the Tall T foreman, was studying the tip of his cigarette, obviously trying to keep from laughing outright. Even Cherry Carr had to grin.

But there was no mirth in Ed Martin's narrow dark eyes. "And since when," he demanded, "did Texas men start driving stockers to Kansas? There ain't a good-sized yearling in your outfit, stranger."

"I guess Texas men," shrugged Hunter, "don't know much about ranching. Stocker, yearling, feeder—they're all cows to us."

It had taken the Sloping S owner a long time to realize that fun was being poked at him. Not a fun-making man himself, he sometimes never recognized humor at all. Now his thick lips went tight and his dark eyes gleamed. Cherry Carr edged even closer to his boss with an expectant grin —trouble was very near, and he liked trouble. Martin would have to back up his talk. Any cattleman would. But the redhead also sensed that Brad Hunter hadn't come this far

4

to turn back. The Texan was not packing a gun, and that would worry him until he found out the reason why.

Neither of the strangers seemed particularly impressed by Ed Martin's mounting anger. For a moment nobody said a word. Beyond Brad Hunter the Tall T riders were milling the cattle in and out in a narrowing circle, as if about to bed them down for the night. Evidently they already had their orders. The three chuck wagons were being drawn up in a semicircle under the shade of tall cottonwoods. Even while they waited stoically for their boss's play, the Wyoming men studied these Texas riders in admiration. That was handling cattle!

"We won't be off by sundown," Brad Hunter said calmly. "If you can prove this is your range, Martin, we'll pay for the grass our cows eat. But a Texas amigo told me this wasn't your range. Said a man named Ed Martin claimed the Sloping S country but didn't have a sheet of paper to prove he owned it. 'Don't pay any attention to this Martin,' my amigo says. Reckon I'll stand pat on that, Martin, until you show me different."

"Then, by God, I'll show you!" cursed Ed. He grabbed for his holster.

Cherry Carr caught his arm and wrestled the gun down. "Ed, you fool!" barked the riding boss. "He ain't armed."

"And there are twenty boys back there who ain't killed nothing but rabbits since leaving Texas, and their trigger fingers are getting itchy," put in Squint Elliott. His leg was still swung over the saddle, but he was tense and his face grim.

Now Martin sullenly replaced the gun in its holster. "Your talk don't make sense to me, stranger," he snapped. "Nor the way you don't pack a gun."

"Not much of a shooting man," shrugged Brad Hunter.

5

During the split second when Cherry had leaped to push down Martin's revolver, he had not stirred in his saddle, even though his eyes had narrowed and his face had paled a little. Now he was calmness personified again.

"If you really own this land," he added, "you don't hafta jerk a gun on me to get me out. My Texas amigo could be wrong. Ain't there a law in Wyoming? If there is, and you got a deed to this grass, I'm guilty of trespassing. Why not let the law handle it, Martin?"

"I don't run to the law to protect what's my own," growled Ed.

"Sometimes it pays," Brad pointed out with a cold grin. "I'm not packing a gun myself, friend. But, like Squint told you, there are twenty boys here who do. Bring your law down here, and we'll listen to it. But any notion you got about playing rough with us is plumb silly, Martin. A twenty-man outfit from Texas ain't still wet behind the ears." His voice was gentle, but the sureness and grimness of his words were unmistakable.

Ed Martin, a cautious man except when flaming-mad, realized that no handful of Sloping S riders would stampede this Texas outfit back over the pass. Now it was his turn to hold Cherry Carr back: the redhead was not angry—he never knew anger; but Cherry never rode away from a challenge, and one had been hurled, even if gently and delicately.

"We'll try the law first," agreed Martin, jerking his foreman's bridle and pulling him back. "You Texans talk big. Mebbe you got twenty fire-eaters like you say. But if the law doesn't get you, Hunter, *I* will."

"Let it lie there," the Texan agreed crisply. "Now, gents, we gotta get back to our camp. Got stew if you're hungry."

"We got grub at our own place," growled Martin.

The Tall T owner shrugged his shoulders and touched spurs to his horse. His foreman followed, leaving the six Sloping S riders to exchange questioning looks, and then to turn upon Ed Martin.

"Say the word, Ed," drawled Cherry, "and we'll salivate that outfit."

"No," Martin answered vigorously. "There is funny business here. Like he said, he has got twenty men. I'll see what the law does."

Cherry's lips crooked. He could see the humor of this—Ed Martin turning to the law for protection. Then, curiously: "Where did he get that stuff about you not owning this grass?" In his lifetime he had never heard the issue raised. He couldn't remember when Jupiter Cross and Sledge Mahoney hadn't conceded to Ed Martin the slopes that fell away from Sunrise Pass into the twisting river bed, including lush spring-fed Frenchman's Creek.

"I dunno," Ed Martin said slowly. The hot anger that had caused him to whip out his gun on Brad Hunter was gone; in its place was a mixture of apprehension and resentment. And a grim determination to play out the hand even if he didn't like his hole card.

He turned in his saddle to glare after the two Texans, then jerked his bridle and spun his horse around on its haunches.

"I'm riding in to see Newt Norton," he announced curtly. "Take the boys and work the north ridges, Cherry."

The redhead's eyes widened. "We won't run into the Texans up there," he murmured. He did not altogether disguise the contempt in his voice. He had a respect for Ed Martin's way of doing things, but not always a liking. Nor would he always cooperate. He would concede Ed's cleverness, but he still liked his own code to live by. Or die by.

"You heard what I said," Ed growled. "I don't want to find a stray up there tomorrow."

Cherry accepted the orders with a shrug.

Brad Hunter and Squint Elliott did not exchange a word until they had returned to the camp under the cottonwoods and were pouring coffee out of the five-gallon camp pot. Then, pushing his hat back on his head and squatting Indian-fashion while he blew into his cup, Squint murmured:

"Podner, that fool notion of yours about not packing hardware is going to get us in a heap of trouble. In the first place, it ain't according to Hoyle. Second, it's plumb unhealthy."

"Could be," Brad murmured; "but them are orders, Squint."

The foreman sighed. "I don't sabby this layout," he murmured. "This valley is bueno, but I've seen prettier ones in Texas."

"It'll make sense sometime," Brad shrugged. "Sit in, and don't challenge the deal, Squint."

"Hell, ain't I sitting? I sat a horse all the way from Texas."

Most of the riders were in camp. With the herd milling in the lush flat around the creek mouth, standing knee-deep in high blue stem, the hard work was over until they took the trail again. The cows would not roam far from grass and water.

"What the boys need," murmured Squint, "is to cut loose their wolf. They got too much money coming to 'em for their own good." And he nodded toward one of the chuck wagons.

Under its shade six of the riders were playing poker with

a frayed worn deck, using matches in lieu of chips. A box of these matches had been soaked with tallow and issued to the boys to use for their poker and blackjack games. Brad would redeem them all when the trail drive was over. It was custom that riders didn't draw their pay until the drive was done.

Squint spoke from experience, and Brad nodded in agreement. Trail riders were a restless lot. Money burned holes in their pockets. Brad and Squint had recruited these men from a dozen Texas towns—San Antonio and Fort Worth and Cotulla and Doan's Crossing. Except for a handful from the Tall T who wanted to accompany the trail herd north, they were drifters from choice. Hunter knew about these exceptions and was not worried. There was a thin line between outlaw and honest rider which more than one honest rider had crossed.

"We got to keep 'em in camp," Brad ordered. "They can go into Shadrock by twos and threes if they don't have whisky money and they promise to stay out of trouble. The man who starts shooting has me to settle with."

"Figger you can stop the shooting?" questioned Squint. "If our boys don't start it, that Sloping S outfit will. That redheaded guy, he looked at you as if he was just itching from trouble."

"We don't want shooting," Brad insisted.

The foreman shrugged his shoulders. "You're forking this bronc'. But your notions don't make sense to me. You wanna move in on a man's range and throw that fact right in his face. I don't think Wyoming men will take that any more than Texas men. I don't know of any way to make notions like that stick except by Sam Colt. And me, I've always been partial to the idea of getting in the first shot."

Brad stood up, emptying his cup of coffee grounds. "I'm

9

riding into town to make a visit to the bank," he announced. "Wanna come along?"

"Without your iron?" Squint asked.

"Yep."

"And seeing the bank? 'Pears like we're gonna stay around here a spell."

"We might," admitted Brad, "be staying a spell."

"Well," sighed Squint, "I've seen worse country. Take Kansas now in the spring. The danged dust is so thick you can't eat anything but hard-boiled eggs. One April day I heard a rustling sound over my head and looked up to see a coyote twenty feet high digging a hole in the ground. And one night . . ."

Chapter Two

NEWT NORTON stepped out of the hotel and surveyed the crooked ribbon of golden dust which was Shadrock's main street with a grimace of distaste. This town sprawled here like a festering sore on the flank of a thick-hided steer, etched on the same pattern as a thousand other western towns, with an outscatter of sheds and corrals at one end and a dust-tired street leading to a green-sprinkled cluster of frame houses at the other.

Then interest leaped into the marshal's eyes. Ed Martin pulled up before the hotel, his horse lathery from sweat, and rolled out of the saddle. Norton sensed the reason for his haste even before the ranchman spoke; but he waited calmly and with great satisfaction. There was not a man, woman, or child in Shadrock who did not know that a trail herd had pushed over the brow of Sunset Pass and camped for the night at the mouth of Frenchman's Creek.

"Marshal, that damned trail herd has bedded down on my grass!" Ed omitted the formality of a greeting. "We rode by, and their ramrod invited me to get the law on 'em. Said if they were trespassing and the law ordered 'em off, they would pull out."

Norton's eyebrows knit in perplexity. That didn't sound like this country. In twenty-five years as marshal of Shadrock—a pensionlike job since the mining boom had died out but once a task that required a man young and fearless—he had never received such a complaint. There was still in this country a feeling that the law had nothing to do with the limits of a man's grass, that God had put it here for the man who could take it and keep it.

"Sure, if that's what they want," Norton said slowly. He did not like Martin, and Martin knew why; but the ranchman paid taxes, and it was the marshal's job to protect the citizens of his township. He studied Ed's sweating dark face. "But it seems to me to be Dugan's job," he murmured.

Dugan was the sheriff and a friend of Ed Martin's. A sheriff necessarily had to be the friend of Martin, Jupiter Cross, and Sledge Mahoney. In every range it was the same, until the big cattlemen clashed among themselves, and then sheriffs were pawns in their game. Newt Norton, as marshal, took orders from no one.

"Dugan can't handle it," Ed Martin answered shortly.

Newt's lips curved in a mirthless smile. Two elections before, Norton had run against Sam Dugan. Martin and the other big outfits had beaten him.

"Besides," the ranchman added, "Dugan is out of town."

Norton nodded. That was true. There was little need for law enforcement in this county. The sheriff was a nonenity as well as a figurehead. Sometimes, in town, a law man had to be on his toes. Riders in on pay day got plenty rough, cutting loose their wolf. Newt usually handled them without trouble. A waddy had to be plenty drunk to get nasty with the marshal.

"I'll ride out and warn 'em they are trespassing," Newt agreed after a moment. "But it's Dugan who'll have to use force on 'em."

"Bueno," nodded Ed. "Dugan won't do anything, of course. Just mouth. If they don't take your orders, we'll handle 'em ourselves. First we want 'em duly notified by law."

Another thin smile from the graven-faced marshal. "That doesn't sound like you, Ed," he murmured, and he went around to the livery stable behind the hotel for his horse.

As he rode toward the creek he saw Martin disappearing into Fatty's bar, and the specks in the distance that were Texas cattle helping themselves to the Sloping S dry range. Ed drank in quick savage gulps, he recalled, and was sometimes rash and headstrong when likkered up. Perhaps the Texans ought to be warned to stay out of town this night.

Then he saw two horsemen coming toward Shadrock. He guessed who they were, straightened his star, pushed back the brim of his weatherbeaten hat, and then waited with as near to a smile on his leathery face as there ever was. The sardonic humor of the situation appealed to him. After these twenty-five years he was having to do an errand for Ed Martin. Even now he could remember facing the ranchman in front of Fatty's, exactly that long ago, and telling him coldly, meaning every word of it: "If I were sheriff instead of marshal, Martin, I would have you under six feet of sod by morning." Martin had seized the Sloping S ranch in flagrant violation of every law there was, even unwritten range law. Yet here that same law had to back Ed's hand.

Twice Newt had stood for sheriff, intending, if elected, to do some investigating into Martin's past. As sheriff he could drag out even an incident twenty-five years old. As marshal he could only sit back and remember.

He was pretty sure Ed Martin had spent some money beating him in his last contest against old wishy-washy Sam Dugan. But it was to Newt Norton that Martin had come pleading for the shelter of the law. Sometimes his was not a pleasant job.

"Howdy, gents," he said as the two Texans pulled up their horses.

"Evening," was the courteous retort.

Newt's star was there in plain sight. "Either of you gents own that herd?" he asked, waving toward the creek.

"Reckon I do," Brad nodded. "Name is Hunter. It's the Tall T brand from Texas."

"It's my duty as an officer," Newt said, "to warn you that you are trespassing on private range. Being as you're a stranger, there won't be any charge filed if you move out your herd right away."

Brad threw his leg across his horse's neck and rolled a cigarette with annoying deliberation. "Reckon you're marshal?" he asked finally.

"Yes," was the quick answer. Norton had been hoping this Texan would know that much law.

"We're not camped in town," was the crisp answer. "Any trouble my boys start in your limits, I'll settle for. They're camped out and I'm riding in without hardware. Don't see how, marshal, you got a kick coming."

Newt's lips tightened, but not from anger. He was trying to suppress a smile. "I'm only warning you," he shrugged. "The sheriff is out of town. Usually I act for him when he's gone. Mebbe the court would decide I'm acting outside my jurisdiction, mebbe not. Custom here would hold me up. And this, friend, is our country."

Brad thought a minute, then conceded that point. "Whose private range are we trespassing on?" he demanded.

"The Sloping S ranch."

"Who owns it?"

"Man by name of Ed Martin."

"Reckon Mr. Martin has his deed filed all legal-like?" Brad Hunter drawled. "Reckon he has gone into court and got a legal complaint drawn up and you're serving papers on us?"

"No," Norton answered. "I'm merely warning you."

"You seem to be taking Ed Martin's word that he owns the Sloping S," Hunter shot back, a crisp tone creeping into his voice, "and that we're on his grass. Suppose you take my word for it that Martin doesn't own it."

"You're challenging Martin's title?" the marshal asked slowly.

"That's right." Brad nodded.

"And my right to order you to leave with your cattle until I am given a court order which necessarily would establish the ownership of the land?"

Newt could have turned and ridden off, but he wanted to go through this formality. Perhaps this stranger's story needed strengthening. Perhaps he didn't know the legal phraseology which would justify his stand. If so, Newt would brush him up on it.

"That's right." Brad nodded again.

Newt turned his horse around. "In that case," he said, "I'll return to Shadrock and tell Martin to ask the sheriff for a legal trespass charge."

"We're riding that way," Brad said. "Mosey along with us."

The three rode abreast on the dusty road. Newt turned in his saddle several times to survey the young Texan who cantered along as if he didn't have a care in the world.

"From Texas you said?" he asked.

"That's right. Down south of San Antone."

"A long way up here for a trail herd," Newt murmured.

"So Martin said," Hunter shrugged. "No law against driving a herd from Texas to Kansas by way of Wyoming, is there?"

"Not that I ever heard of," the marshal admitted with that telltale tightening of his lips. "But it's plumb peculiar. Makes folks want to ask questions."

"Go ahead, if they're not too personal," the Texan invited.

"Who gave you the idea that the mouth of Frenchman's Creek was open range? and that Ed Martin hasn't got a deed to the Sloping S on file at the courthouse?"

"Oh, talk got around," was the careless answer. "They said down in Texas that nobody ever legally bought the creek mouth, that the Sloping S just got in the habit of using it—but that a homesteader named Calvin Kimberlin had lived on the place a long time, and that his homestead claim would stand up against all comers if he ever took the notion to file it."

"You seem to know this country," Newt said slowly. There was a faint gleam deep back in his eyes. "Who passed along talk like that?"

He leaned forward a little in his saddle, waiting impatiently for an answer. For a moment it looked as if there would be no reply. Then the Texan said, with seeming reluctance:

"A drifting fellow who used to operate out of here. Called himself Drifting Dan Thompson."

Again there was a quick movement of Newt Norton's lips, as if the impassive mask that was his face were about to crack into a million pieces. But again he got himself under control quickly.

"Seems like I remember something about Drifting Dan," he nodded.

They came into town at this same lazy lope. The elm-shaded courthouse was beyond the saloon, and cater-cornered across from the frame building which accommodated

16

Shadrock's only bank, the post office, and the town's biggest store, which sold everything from groceries to women's silk dresses and mail-order saddles. A painted sign dulled with the years announced that this was Luther Coleman's property. The Texans pulled up their horses.

"Gotta pay a call here," Brad explained. "I'll be hanging around the saloon for a while. Be glad to see you later and chin with you some."

"May be around," Newt nodded.

He could see Ed Martin in front of Fatty's, watching intently. He rode on to the courthouse and started up the steps. He was halted by a shout behind him.

The Sloping S owner was coming across the street on the double-quick.

"Well?" he demanded impatiently.

Again Norton's face threatened to splatter into a smile. "The Texan says there never was any ownership of the creek mouth," he explained coldly. "Said it is still government land and would belong to Cal Kimberlin by squatter's rights if Cal claimed it. He also challenged your ownership to the Sloping S. Said to bring your deed into court and get a legal trespass order."

The look on Martin's face brought a gleam into the marshal's eyes, but otherwise he curtailed his glee. These men were not simply unfriendly; Newt Norton nourished a memory which had developed with the passing thwarted years into a personal grudge.

"Is your deed on file, Martin?"

"Hell, no!" Ed Martin snorted. "How many deeds are on file in there?" and he waved toward the clerk's office.

"There has to be one," Norton pointed out. "I happen to recall that Bill Bradley bought the Sloping S. Then the Crazy N. Those brands, together with ownership, were duly registered. What have you got to show for your possession?"

"A bill of sale," Martin snapped. He did not conceal his hesitancy very well. "It's down at Luke Coleman's bank," he said after a moment.

"I see," murmured Newt. He did not believe it. Not for a long time had Ed Martin done business with Luther Coleman's bank.

He leaned against the banister and rolled a smoke. "I'll serve papers in Sam Dugan's absence," he stated coldly, "but only if they're legally drawn up. Better see the judge if you want me to do anything."

"Sure," Ed agreed. All too amiably—it was obvious that his mind was wandering. "I'll see Coleman right away."

He turned back to the bank. The two Texans were inside talking to the blonde girl who was Luther Coleman's niece. Ed took his post across the street, watching with narrow eyes and tight lips. His right hand hovered close to the butt of his gun. Through the plate-glass window he could see everything that was going on. The banker wasn't in sight, and he hoped he was dead-drunk as usual. The Texans could talk to the girl all they wanted to.

Grace Coleman was wiping the store counter when Brad Hunter and Squint Elliott entered. Womanlike, she pretended that she had not noticed them. Of course she had, and had known them right off as bosses of the trail herd which had trickled over the pass to set Shadrock a-buzzing with rumors and speculation.

She could have easily been a pretty girl. That she was not was due to a woman's unvarying stubbornness against the transition which this country demanded of humans, or else. Man had yielded to this new raw land's rugged forces,

18

changing even his clothes and his type of saddle and his manner of riding, holding, perhaps, no more than a semblance of his personality. But woman, unyielding, unprotesting, after a half-century still tried to bring across the barrier the beauty and the way of life that her mother and grandmother had known, even while common sense told her that this out-of-place way would not, against this background, be beautiful at all.

What Grace Coleman lacked, as she raised inquiring eyes and regarded Brad Hunter with quickening interest, was what a young woman of her age across that divide could have had for the asking, and which here was unobtainable —an artificiality of color, a harmony of dress pattern, a coolness even when the day was hot, a self-assured aloofness from the humdrum of material things. Here, even in July's blistering heat, Grace wore many petticoats and a calico dress, because woman would not leave her way of dressing behind, and her blond ringlets fell limp around her shoulders because it was time-old that a girl's hair must curl, and beads of perspiration on her forehead gave a certain coarseness to her complexion, for a lady must not permit her cheeks to be sun-tanned and hardened.

There was also a weariness about her which had nothing to do with the physical aspects of this country, a drabness which came from within and which was even grayer than the monotony embracing her from without.

But yet, to Brad Hunter, she seemed far from commonplace, for she was a woman and this was a landscape practically untouched by a woman's hand. He stared at her a moment before lifting his hat, and the things she suddenly remembered—her overdamp face and her stained hands and her askew curls—made her seem even more attractive to a man who had looked upon nothing but dance-hall girls for a long time, and was heart-sick from an overdose of artificiality.

"Yes?" she asked with dignity, impersonally.

"Howdy, ma'm," Brad grinned, and for the first time she heard the speech, musical and slow, of a man from the deep South. (Wyoming men talked in a confused pattern, without a distinctive dialect or drawl.) "I'd like to see Mr. Luther Coleman."

"I'm in charge of the bank. I'm his niece."

"Mr. Coleman isn't here?"

"No."

"When do you expect him?"

"At no certain time," she said a little irritably. She had gone over this so many times before. It was always surprising to strangers that Shadrock's banking and post-office business was conducted by a girl. Shadrock had learned to wait until Luther Coleman was out of sight, preferring to deal with his niece; but newcomers always liked to deal with a man.

Brad frowned. Grace Coleman took advantage of his hesitation to study his face. If there was a boldness, and a too-quick selfish curiosity, in her surveillance, it was because any young woman in this country had learned that coyness might be her daily role, but boldness was advisable if and when her moment, and her man, came along. Boys and girls grew up entirely too young in this region, the girls in such a rush that none of them were ever completely reconciled to it. A boy could do a man's work and still be young; but youth and gayety and a woman's job were irreconcilable.

Brad had the leanness and sharpness of features she had seen in other men—he was of a general pattern into which most western men fell; but she saw by the cut of his chin and the tilt of his head that he was not an everyday line rider. He either was something else, or would be soon, come hell or high water. Her eyes roved down to his belt and, with a start, she realized that he was unarmed. The Texan with him, silent and squint-eyed, wore the proverbial pistol hanging low, but this younger man did not have even a gun belt.

Thus was the first flicker of interest stirred in Grace Coleman by Brad Hunter, up from Texas. Others would speculate as to why this lean young man "parked his hardware." Grace, who had spent eight years in the East, who was held in this Wyoming country by loyalty to a man she did not actually love, warmed to the newcomer because of this odd omission of a weapon. It suggested that he might have gentleness and character and understanding, none of which she had been able to find in the range men who came to "spark" her whenever she would permit—the son of Jupiter Cross, and Sledge Mahoney just after his wife's death.

"I'm Brad Hunter of Texas," he explained. "I'm driving a herd of cattle to market, the Tall T brand. I wanted to deposit some money with Mr. Coleman. And an important paper."

"I'll be glad to accept it," Grace answered quietly. "I'm in charge of the bank when my uncle is out."

"Your uncle?"

"Yes, uncle."

He gave her a quick searching look. "You weren't raised here?" From his tone he already knew the answer; it was more of a statement than a question.

"Is that necessary, Mr. Hunter?" she demanded with dignity. She could not understand her sudden blaze of anger at his curiosity. She wanted him to be curious. But the habits of long years are not easily laid aside. For a long time Grace Coleman had worn a chip on her shoulder for the curious men of Shadrock and the neighboring Wyoming valleys to slap at if they wished.

"I would prefer," Brad said quietly, "to do business with Mr. Coleman himself. If you will tell me when you expect him back, I'll mosey along and return later."

"There is no telling," she shrugged. "I have handled all of the bank's business for the past two months."

Which was true. Not in that time, as the Shadrock gossips well knew, had Luther Coleman "drawn a sober breath."

Brad hesitated again. Then, obviously unwilling, he reached into a hip pocket and drew out a thick leather wallet.

"Here is ten thousand dollars in currency," he explained, "and a valuable deed. I'd like to leave them here on deposit."

She took pencil and paper and wrote out a deposit slip. He signed a card and then shocked her with his next question.

"Do you know a Calvin Kimberlin?"

"Why, yes, of course." Everyone in Shadrock knew Cal. And broad rough-talking Maude, his wife.

"And a lady named Ramona Custer?"

Grace Coleman's lips tightened, and a spot of red appeared in each cheek. Also was Ramona known.

"I know Miss Custer by sight," she said stiffly.

A glint of amusement came into Brad Hunter's eyes. "I see," he smiled. "I asked because I wanted to leave instructions for the disposition of this deed and money if I should fail to claim them in a year's time. I wish the deed to become the property of Calvin and Maude Kimberlin. And the money to go to Miss Ramona Custer. You are authorized to make payment to them at one year from date, with or without their request or knowledge. You will want that in writing, of course."

"Of course," she nodded, and began to scratch away with her pen, putting his words into the best legal language she knew.

As she wrote, her thoughts were weaving a framework of curious questions she would have to learn the answers to, if he stayed in Shadrock that long. It was curious that this man from Texas should ride into Shadrock, obviously making the bank his first stop, and talk glibly of Shadrock people—asking for her uncle by name, assigning a deed to Calvin and Maude Kimberlin, leaving instructions for the payment of ten thousand dollars in cash to Ramona Custer if he should not return within a year's time.

"Is that all?" she asked finally.

He hesitated. She looked up, and was a little taken back by the hardness in his face.

"No," he said. "Give my regards to your uncle. Tell him his bank was recommended to me by a man who used to live around these parts—a man called Drifting Dan Thompson."

Grace Coleman had never heard the name before. She nodded. "I'll tell Uncle Luke," she promised.

"The deed," Brad said slowly, "is more important than the money. Take no chances with it."

"It'll be here when you return," she said crisply.

"Thank you. So long, ma'm."

He tipped his hat, as did his squint-eyed companion, who had not spoken a single word all this time. She looked after him a moment and not even Grace Coleman herself knew what she felt. Shadrock spoke of her as a man hater—and she had been that to Shadrock men who had tried to pay her court. Which included practically all the eligible ones and a few married men who sometimes drank too much, and forgot the consequences. There would never be enough women in this country for all the men. Not all the women who came would live. Some would die before their husbands, as Theresa Coleman, the wife of Luther Coleman and Grace's aunt, had died. Of a heart that was broken and crushed.

Chapter Three

ED MARTIN waited until Brad and Squint had walked down the street and disappeared into Fatty's saloon. Then he entered the bank.

Grace Coleman had just completed her notations on this new strange account and was placing the wallet, and her notes, in the ancient iron safe which was partitioned off from the rest of the building by a railing.

"Is Luke in?" he demanded when she looked up.

"I don't know," Grace answered curtly. She had never learned what there was between her uncle and Ed Martin to make Luther Coleman despise the Sloping S owner, and obviously fear him, but she heartily concurred in the sentiment.

"I want to see him."

"I don't think he wants to see you," she shot back. Uncle Luke had given her instructions never to let Ed Martin in to see him. This was one order she was willing to obey.

Martin's eyes blazed at her. "Look, girl," he said roughly. "This is important. I'm gonna see Luke if I have to tear this joint apart."

Before Grace could answer, a voice called from behind the partition:

"Who is it, honey?"

The ranchman answered for himself. "Ed Martin, Luke. I gotta see you."

"No," was the quick retort. There was a note of fright in the voice from behind the wall. Luther Coleman never tried to conceal the fact that he hated Ed Martin, or that he was afraid of him.

"I'm going in," Ed told Grace, pushing open the gate. "Sorry to act impolite, but it's important. When Luke knows what it's all about, he'll be glad to talk to me."

Coleman's niece hesitated. Then, with a resigned shrug, she turned her back to her work. Already the man was by her. She could not stop him if she tried. He was powerful and could thrust her aside with one sweep of his arm—and, she knew, would do it without a qualm. Nobody had ever accused Ed Martin of being gentle or courteous.

She heard her uncle's voice, suddenly shrill, as if frightened. "Dang it, Ed, I warned you once—"

Martin interrupted, his voice a low snarl. "Shut up, you sniveling fool. Do you want the whole town in on it?"

Then the door slammed shut behind the Sloping S owner, and Grace could hear only snatches of their talk.

"You gotta swear there is a deed and it's in your vault," Ed Martin was insisting. "Dugan, damn him, won't be back for a week. Till then, we gotta deal with Norton."

"I ain't doing it," the banker avowed.

"You're in this with me," Martin said warningly.

Grace tried not to listen. She was not interested in her uncle's business, even though she did the actual running of it. She heard Ed's rough laugh and then her uncle's threatening voice:

"See this shotgun, Ed. I'll use it on you some day. Heaven help me, I'll blast you with it if you ever step into this place again."

She leaped up, startled and frightened. She had never

26

considered her uncle as a man of violence. Other men in Shadrock wore guns low, and used them quickly and efficiently. But not Luther Coleman, who wore black broadcloth suits and white shirts and who, in recent years, had drunk from one dawn to the next. One could not imagine a more harmless man.

Through the plate-glass window she sighted Newt Norton. The marshal had seen Hunter and Elliott go into Fatty's bar. And Ed Martin wait until they had left the bank, then enter it almost on their heels. A puzzle that Newt Norton had not thought about in many years was now piecing itself out in his mind. And he was enjoying it. A man who has nourished a hate for twenty-five years necessarily gloats in seeing that dormant hatred come back to life. It pleased Newt Norton that at long last Ed Martin's chickens were coming home to roost.

Grace ran out into the street and called the law man. She explained that Ed Martin had forced his way into their living quarters and that she had heard her uncle threaten the Sloping S owner with his shotgun.

"Uncle Luke might kill him!" she wailed.

Strange to say, that was what she was afraid of. Newt almost grinned: If anybody was in danger of being killed, it was Luke Coleman; as for Luke killing Martin . . .

"I'd be an unpopular man if I stopped that," he sighed, "but I'll see what I can do."

As he pushed the swinging gate in the three-quarters partition and started into the living quarters he met Ed Martin coming out. Martin's black glance leaped with quick accusation to Grace's face.

"Well?" he demanded, turning back to the marshal.

"Any trouble here?"

"Not that I know of," Martin snapped. "Just talking to

Coleman, that's all. That ain't part of a marshal's business, is it?"

Now Luther Coleman appeared. Though he was not an old man—no older than Martin or Norton, anyhow—his hair was white and his body sparse and decrepit. His faded eyes met Norton's questioning gaze, and he nodded.

"Yeah, just talking," he muttered. But he didn't have Ed's assurance. He didn't want to meet the marshal's eyes.

"I see," Newt said slowly. He lifted his hat and turned back to the street.

He turned at the deserted blacksmith's shop just across from Coleman's building and saw Ed Martin walking toward Fatty's. The two Texans were evidently still there—their horses were hitched in front. Newt walked slowly back in that direction. He knew Ed Martin for a man of sudden angry violence. Until he lost his temper, Ed was cunning and was dangerous for what he might do under cover. When his anger ran hot he wasn't a clever man. Then he seemed possessed of the idea that he might bulldoze his way through.

The Texans were still in the saloon. One of them, the man who was doing the talking, who had ordered his trail herd to pitch camp on Ed Martin's range, didn't wear a gun. Newt didn't like that, and quickened his steps. Ed Martin would shoot down an unarmed man if in the mood.

The Sloping S owner could hardly see a foot in front of him because of that blinding rage which Newt had noticed. Martin could lay out a pattern, an orderly pattern, and he could push through his deals with insistent force; but if something broke that pattern he was no smarter than the next man. Actually he didn't see Calvin Kimberlin turn his creaking wagon in to the sidewalk and climb out of the seat with the stiffness of a man who is old, and has an old man's miseries. Perhaps he wouldn't have turned aside if he had seen Calvin turn down the street, right in his path. He crashed into the gaunt homesteader whose tired ageless face was as much of the valley's changeless pattern as the lofty Sunrise Pass, and his shoulder caught Kimberlin squarely, knocking the nester off balance. As he stalked on, never looking back, immediately a small crowd of cowmen appeared in front of the saloon, watching with a narrow amusement. Kimberlin got up from the dirt and stood still a moment, staring at his feet.

In the wagon Maude Kimberlin rolled to her feet after a laborious struggle, the creaking of the seat springs as her weight left it drowning out all other sounds.

"Ed Martin, you'll lay a hand on him once too often!" she called after the ranchman, who didn't seem to hear.

Calvin Kimberlin must cower before rough range men—but not his wife, not Maude Kimberlin who weighed over two hundred pounds and who had the sharpest tongue in the valley. With a grumble she sat back again, and the springs squeaked protestingly.

"Aw, Maw, it's all right. He didn't hurt Paw any."

The protest came from a round-faced, wide-eyed girl who sat by her, squeezed tight against the side of the seat by her mother's broadness. This was Catherine Kimberlin, the nester's daughter. Under her broad bonnet her eyes were wide and curious as she looked at the men in front of the saloon, who quickly checked their laughter under her glance. One of them even lifted his hat. This was a Sloping S rider, Jinx Duval. As he turned off he muttered to his companion, one of Jupiter Cross's men:

"Cherry oughta be in town to see his lady love."

"Cherry likes to see 'em by the dark of the moon," was the grinning retort.

Catherine Kimberlin did not hear their speech; but she did catch their laughter, and she reddened. There was about her a prettiness which other men in the valley besides Cherry Carr had commented upon. Perhaps in time she would have the weight and coarseness of her mother; but now, in the first full flush of youth, she was, in Cherry's words, "as plump as a butter ball and just as sweet."

Now her father came out of the saddle shop and walked on to Coleman's corner building. Maude took up the reins, and the team of tired horses pulled the equally tired wagon after him.

Behind them Ed Martin opened the door of the saloon and shot a quick look inside. He saw Brad Hunter and Squint Elliott at a table with two of Jupiter Cross's cowboys. He let the door go and stood in the shade of the building picking at his stained teeth with the stem of a match. The rush of his hot anger had faded, and he was thinking things out.

Newt Norton now had sauntered up.

"Kinda hot," sighed the marshal. "If you got the makings, Ed, I'll roll a smoke."

Martin's eyes flashed. The law man usually smoked cigars, and a request from him for the makings was merely an excuse to hang around.

"Sometimes, Newt," he growled, "marshals can get in the way."

"And sometimes," Newt said coldly, "they come in powerful handy. If you got any ideas about shooting an unarmed man, Ed, forget 'em."

"Who's to stop me?" Martin flared.

The marshal's lips quirked downward, and he gave the Sloping S owner a long steady look.

"Twenty-five years ago," he murmured, "I was looking

for a chance to pull on you. I ain't found it yet, but I'm still looking."

The two Jupiter Cross riders were at the bar when Brad and Squint came up. Brad gave them a pleasant nod and motioned to their half-empty glasses.

"Half-sole 'em, gents," he invited. "Texas cowboys get thirsty just like Wyoming men."

Jupiter Cross, the white-haired owner of the Cross brand, swore these two cowboys were the sorriest in all of Wyoming. They were—except in work seasons. Chuckling Charley Cox could hold a job because he could fork a bolt of lightning. Maggie Stevens looked like a barrel of fat; but it was all solid clear through, and he could manhandle a six-months dogie with his left hand and slap on a brand with his right. Prime roundup men, both of them. Jupiter could well afford to put up with their too-frequent falls from grace during the off season.

Charlie and Maggie exchanged glances, then nodded. "My handle is Cox. They call me 'Chuckling Charley,'" he volunteered, and showed how he had received his nickname. "This overpastured gent is named Mortimer Stevens. He thinks Mortimer is sissy; so, to keep on the good side of him, we called him 'Maggie.'"

"Hunter, Brad Hunter. This is my range boss, Squint Elliott. His eyes got that way gawking at the pretty gals at Fort Laramie."

The barkeep handed over the bottle, and Hunter poured the drinks himself. The two Cross riders regarded him with open thoughtfulness and curiosity.

"You're kind of a button to be owning a spread like that," murmured Chuckling Charley.

"Inherited it," Brad shrugged.

31

"We're from the Cross," volunteered Maggie. "Jupiter's outfit. Mebbe you've heard of it."

"Some," admitted Brad. "You run up the slope to Ed Martin's Sloping S and back across the foothills to Sledge Mahoney's. Some good grass in there."

"Yeah," nodded Charley. It struck both cowboys at the same time that this stranger from Texas had good insight into valley affairs.

"He's full of stuff like that," grinned Squint, jerking his head toward his boss. "Knows all sorts of things. Can even read."

"I could once," sighed Charley. "But they seem to have changed the alphabet since I was a button. Last letter I got, I couldn't make heads nor tails of it."

"You sheep-dipper, you never got a letter in your life," charged Maggie.

"He's always running me down," sighed Charley. "I steer him out of trouble and break every cayuse he rides. Hafta get 'em plumb gentle, too. He can't stay on an honest-to-goodness cow pony."

Brad motioned to one of the round tables which littered the saloon. On pay days Fatty did a good business with his poker games. "I get kinda tired standing up. Suppose we sit and chew the fat?"

"It takes longer between drinks when you're sitting down," pointed out Charley.

"Not," grinned Brad, "if you carry the bottle with you."

The four of them settled in cane-bottomed chairs, and Maggie Stevens tilted his seat back against the wall and grinned at his newly found friends.

"Most folks were right peeved when they saw your trail herd coming through the pass," he told Hunter. "But me and Charley, we're kinda glad you moseyed up in this direction. Never such poor drinkers as they got around here."

"Of course," added Charley, "we didn't like your heading for the bank right off. We don't like strangers going into the bank a-tall. It ain't safe, either. In case Miss Grace should take a fancy to you, we couldn't do anything else but salivate you with good hot lead. Most of the things in this he-man's country you can have for the asking; but Miss Grace is something special, and we wouldn't stand for her riding off with a no-good cowpoke."

"No chance of that," shrugged Brad. "I'll promise not to throw a single loop."

"Don't let him bull you," gibed Squint. "Women fall for him like a ton of brick. There was a whole remuda of 'em lined up along the trail when we took off from Texas."

"What kind of country is Texas?"

"Best in the world," Squint said quickly. "Down there men are so tough they comb their hair with a wagon wheel and shave with a hand ax. And the blue stem grows so deep that one spring we lost a hundred calves right in our branding pasture and didn't find 'em again until they were yearlings weighing two thousand pounds per head."

"Two thousand pounds!" murmured Charley.

"That's right."

Chuckling Charley shook his head. "Texas must be *some* place. Why should anybody pull out of Texas and come to Wyoming?"

"Just passing through," explained Brad. "Just driving our herd to market."

"Didn't know," said Charley, "the railroad had gotten out this far. Hear talk about it all time, but last spring we had to go plumb to Ellsworth."

"Figger we'll pick Ellsworth," said Brad. "Dodge City ain't so hot. My boys wanna kick up their heels."

"This," pointed out Charley, "is a long way from Ellsworth. I come up from Texas once. From the Pecos country. But we didn't come by way of Wyoming."

"Every man," grinned Brad, "to his own trail. Let's fill 'em up again, gents."

"Sure, sure," Maggie said quickly. "My turn to buy, gents."

"Likker is on me," Hunter said firmly. "We wanna get along in this country. A man who doesn't pack a gun has to buy the likker."

"Noticed that," murmured Charley. "Don't you feel plumb naked without a gun?"

"Never use 'em," Brad said. "We're as peaceable as Comanches the day before a pack train comes to the reservation."

He also leaned back in his chair. "I'd like to meet your boss sometime. Heard about him from a guy in Texas who knew Jupiter real well."

"Yeah?"

"Called himself Drifting Dan Thompson. Ever hear of him?"

"Some," Maggie admitted, his eyes as bright as coals.

"Wasn't Jupiter a partner of his?"

"Me, I'm just a rider," shrugged Maggie. "I don't try to find out who are a man's friends, and who ain't. Jupiter is a good man to ride the river with. Except for some of his notions, he's a good man to work for. I wouldn't know what he thought—about Drifting Dan Thompson."

"I see," nodded Brad. He reached for the bottle again, but Charley held up a protesting head.

"We gotta ride," he explained. "Jupiter will be mad as a steer who ran into a barbed-wire fence now."

"One other thing," Brad said. "Where do we find this Ramona Custer?"

This question, Jupiter Cross's men could answer. "So you heard about Ramona?" chuckled Charley. "Just start toward the river and keep walking, friend. Either Ramona or her girl will give you a hail from her house. Times are bad up here with so many men married off, and Ramona ain't got the house she used to have. But you'll get a run for your money. The half-breed she's got there ain't hard to look at, and Ramona is some gal herself considering how long she's been around."

"Thanks," grinned Brad.

He and Squint followed the two Cross riders outside.

"That makes a couple of times you mentioned Drifting Dan," murmured Squint. "It sure seems to make an impression on folks around here. I didn't realize the old boy left such a rep behind him."

"Dan was a heller in his time," Brad grinned. "Have we got time for another call, or had we better mosey on back?"

Before Squint could answer, Ed Martin stepped forward, right in their path. Newt Norton was not a pace away.

"Howdy, gents," Brad nodded.

"A word with you, Hunter," growled Martin.

"Sure."

The ranchman stood with his shoulders dropped, unmistakably poised for action. It had taken him a long time to reach this decision. It was not the way he would have chosen to handle the matter; but with only Luke Coleman's half-hearted promise to swear there was a deed to the Sloping S in his vault, with the odds against him if he started a range war, this seemed to be his best bet.

"You want my ranch, Hunter?" he growled. "Is that the way Texans do things—just move in?"

"Isn't that the way you got it?" Brad shot back.

His voice was like the crack of a whip. Ed Martin stiffened. "How do you know how I got it?" he demanded hoarsely.

"I hear things," Brad shrugged. "What else, Martin? I'm in a hurry."

Ed's rushing anger had conquered his judgment again. He snarled and reached for his gun. A second time he was stopped from pulling upon Brad Hunter—this time by Newt Norton.

"I told you, Ed," snapped Newt. "He ain't packing a gun."

"Then let him get one," flared Ed, struggling free. "Let him stand up man to man and make his play. Right now, Hunter, or any time you say. Let's see the color of your backbone."

There was a scuffling sound. Men had gathered quickly around the saloon door; now they were moving back. Never in this country had one man talked like that to another, and both lived. The Texan called Squint started forward, but Brad held him back.

Newt Norton turned to the Tall T owner. "Seems like he makes it pretty clear, friend," murmured the marshal. "Your move now."

"One more threat like that," Brad told Ed, "and I'll have you put under peace bond."

"You mean," croaked Martin, "you ain't going for your gun!"

There was a little of relief in his voice. Ed Martin didn't like this way of settling disputes either.

"I'm not," Brad snapped. "What's between you and me has to be settled some other way."

With that he turned on his heel and stalked to his horse. Squint followed, lips working.

"Brad, podner," appealed the Tall T foreman, "don't take that kind of talk. If you don't want him, lemme have him."

"Come along, Squint," was the cold answer as Brad swung into his saddle.

"But, podner, you can't just ride away from a play like that. I can't figger it out."

Brad touched spurs to his horse and was already gone done the street.

Behind him Ed Martin and Newt Norton regarded each other in amazement.

"I never figgered," Ed said slowly, "I would get by with it. I had the notion he was a hellion."

A grunt was the marshal's answer. He had had the same idea. And his was a savage disappointment it would take a drink to soothe. He turned into the saloon for it.

Squint finally caught up with his boss. "I'm sorry I shot off my mouth, podner," he apologized. "But I got red-hot."

"So did I," answered Brad with a mirthless smile.

They loped to where the Tall T's trail wagons were drawn up on a sandy slope facing Frenchman's Creek. Only four riders were posted for night watch, and the other hands were skylarking like schoolboys. Behind them lay two hard months—never had a trail herd been driven so far, vowed Pecos Pete Campbell, who had been from Texas to Kansas so many times that he could point a herd in his sleep.

The riders swooped down upon Brad, demanding to know how long they would rust their bottoms here in the middle of nowhere. They wanted to press on to Ellsworth.

Brad took a deep breath. He would have more explaining to do when they got the story of how he had backed down before Ed Martin.

"Men," he said slowly, "we've reached the end of the

37

trail—for a while. I told you back in Texas that this would be a crazy sort of drive, that we were trailing to Ellsworth by way of Wyoming. I'd like to give you my reasons. We've ridden rivers together, and I'd trust any one of you with my best saddle. But this is a loco game. I got to play this hand without showing my hole card. You'll get your pay; I'm good for that, and you know it."

Spoke up Pecos, a wrinkle-faced cowman who had worked for a dozen outfits:

"Nobody is backing you to the wall, Brad. We're fidgeting a little mebbe. But we can sit pat until the end of the deal."

"Good. We'll be at Shadrock some time. I can't say how long. You boys have gotta step a narrow line while we're here. I'm gonna try and keep out of trouble. Mebbe I can't. Those men I palavered with this afternoon—they're Sloping S men. They claim this land. I think, if they wanna start something, we can finish it."

"We shore can," murmured another Tall T rider. Brad Hunter had warned them in Texas there might be shooting along this trail. He was paying them to take their chances. Not a man of them had any intention of checking out.

"Every man is to keep close to camp," Brad ordered. "Don't go into town at all without asking me or Squint. When you go, go in twos and threes and don't stay long. Pay for your drinks when they're served, and don't take too many. Any trouble that starts in Shadrock is on your head."

"Godamighty, we'll be going to Sunday school next," grumbled Pecos.

Brad broke up the talk with a wave of his hand, and he and Squint returned to their perch against the front wheel of Limpy's chuck wagon. The cook seemed to be in good spirits, for he brought them coffee. And then sang out "Come and git it" and beamed at the ejaculations of surprise and contentment when the riders saw what would be their fare: small round fillets tossed into smoking fat, pickles, onions, sourdough bread. The Tall T always fed better than most outfits. Limpy would put on the dog during this enforced dull stay at Shadrock.

There was a stirring at one of the outer fires, and Pecos slouched over to the chuck wagon followed by a thin sallow-faced youngster who wore dirty Levis and overrun boots.

"Button to see you, Brad."

Hunter studied the youngster, still in his teens; but there was a cocksure air about him and a defiant tilt to his young head. Brad's eyes dropped to the two guns hanging low in worn holsters. Probably this button could use them.

"Yes?"

"You ramrodding this outfit?"

"Reckon so."

"I'm drifting through. Looking for an outfit to tie up with."

"Where you from?"

"Back yonder," the kid answered curtly, waving toward the pass. "Not that it makes any difference." His voice was curt and challenging.

Brad grinned. "Not a bit," he agreed. He hesitated. If there was anything he didn't need at the moment, it was another hand. There were already a score of restless riders itching to break the monotony of the days ahead with some kind of action. But the kid's face looked pinched. Probably hadn't had a square meal in days.

"We're full up," Brad said apologetically. "But hang around a few days if you feel like it. Plenty of chuck and

39

blankets. Help the boys with the remuda if you wanna work for your keep."

The young face twitched. Obviously this wasn't what he wanted. He started to refuse indignantly, then considered. The smell of hot coffee was tempting, and the aroma of food from Limpy's wagon conquered his pride.

"I'll give you a jump while I'm looking around," he stated with dignity.

"Sure," grinned Brad. "You can help plenty with the horses. They haven't been ridden enough lately, and some of 'em are frisky. See Limpy about a blanket roll."

"Bueno," nodded the youngster.

"What's your handle?" Brad asked.

The kid hesitated. His lips creased in a defiant grin. "Montana is enough, ain't it?"

"Enough for me," shrugged the Tall T owner. "Just something to call a man by."

Chapter Four

CALVIN KIMBERLIN came into the Coleman store, moving with a tired spiritless shamble. Shadrock could not remember him when he had looked any different. He was older than Maude, his wife. He had looked this old when he brought Maude to this valley after his first wife's death. At the time people had wondered what even a woman like Maude could see in such a man.

"Howdy, Miss Grace," he murmured.

She returned his greeting, and he stood there, ill at ease, awkwardly twirling his worn hat around and around in his hands.

"What is it, Calvin?" she asked wearily. "Your credit is still good if that's what you want to know."

"That's fine," he nodded, a fleeting spark of brightness in his eyes. "I can take care of my bill before long, Miss Grace, honest I can. I got nearly a hundred cedar posts cut, and either the Sloping S or Jupiter Cross will need 'em this fall."

"Don't worry about it, Calvin," she said. "Let's have your order."

Maude Kimberlin always made out the list, but she left it to Calvin to come into the store and plead for credit. In that sense Maude was not a typical nester's wife. Her husband might cringe, but not she. Grace deciphered the big woman's scrawl: salt, sugar, coffee. She got the items down

41

from the shelves and put them into an emptied apple box. Then she brought out a bolt of gingham cloth.

"We just got this in, Calvin. I'm sure Mrs. Kimberlin and Katie could use a new dress."

"Reckon they could," Calvin said gratefully. "Cut off what you think we'll need, Miss Grace."

Grace took the scissors and snipped off far more than would be needed for two dresses. Perhaps Maude could take the remnants and make curtains. Calvin expressed his embarrassed thanks and carried off his purchases.

She turned to her books. Faithfully, though with a smile for her trouble, she entered the total amount against Calvin's account. Kimberlin's bill was already higher than he would ever pay, but this was one instance in which she did not follow her uncle's instructions.

Luther now called out from the back room.

"Wasn't that Cal Kimberlin?"

"Yes."

"What did he buy? Grace, you didn't give that trifling nester any more credit, did you?"

"He paid cash, Uncle Luther," the girl lied. She was safe in her story. Luther Coleman never examined the books any more.

"Where did he get it?"

"I didn't ask him that," was the weary reply. "Would you like some dinner?"

"No, thanks, honey. I don't feel so good today. Miseries got me."

Grace pushed back her hair and stepped outside. The coolness of evening was a promise held out to heat-weary tired people. Shadrock was stirring out of its midafternoon languor. The rickety wagon bearing Calvin, Catherine, and Maude Kimberlin was rolling away from the sidewalk. A cloud of dust floated up from the hoofs of a black horse traveling at a breakneck pace: Cherry Carr was riding in from the Sloping S, pulling up with a flourish before the wagon, and grinning down at Catherine Kimberlin.

"Howdy," he said.

But the redhead's bright eyes roving over the girl's full figure said a lot more. They challenged her with an insolent confidence, and laughed at her parents for their reproving frowns.

"Howdy, Cherry Carr," Maude Kimberlin said curtly. "You can tell that boss of yours to leave my man alone. The next time he touches Cal I'm taking an ax handle to him."

"Ed doesn't listen to me much," shrugged Cherry. "Besides, he doesn't mean anything. Tell you what, I'll bring over a side of bacon some night."

His glance had never left Katie's face. He made no effort to conceal the motive behind his offer. Cherry Carr was like that, open with his play.

"Hmph," snorted Maude. "Reckon you can ride over in the daytime just as well."

"Daytime I work for Ed Martin," shrugged Cherry, riding on with a grin. He already had his answer. Katie Kimberlin, without saying a word, had issued him his invitation. When he came over, she would see him.

He dismounted almost at Grace Coleman's feet, tipped his hat, and swept her with his bold eyes.

"My, you look plumb sweet today," he murmured.

"Thank you, Cherry."

He jerked his thumb toward the store. "If you got anything there as sweet as you," he said, "I want it wrapped up."

His bright look was the same, but there was a difference

in his tone. He hadn't spoken to Katie Kimberlin like this. Grace Coleman was not the type of young woman who would fall for him, and he knew it. He even sensed that she came very near despising him. These periodical advances to Luther Coleman's niece were not made with the careless assurance with which he greeted other valley girls, but in a teasing, bantering tone.

"Some day you'll get lonesome," he grinned as she was silent, "and you'll wish you could see old Cherry riding in from the range. So long."

Grace could not help hating what he stood for, but she looked after him with a twinkle in her eyes. Cherry at least had the gift of honesty—his kind of honesty. And one had to envy him that infectious bubbling grin, even if sometimes he was laughing at the wrong things. It was impossible to reconcile that grin with the kind of man he was; but many things in this country were impossible.

She watched him out of sight before going back into the store. Luther Coleman was at his desk thumbing through the mail that had come on the stage two days before.

"Have you had anything to eat?" she asked coldly.

"No. Just a cup of coffee, honey. Black coffee."

Grace gave him an unsympathetic look and swept by his desk into the rear of the building. Many years before, Luther Coleman had built this combination of a home and a business, and had moved into it his wife and small son. Both had since died: the child, of a rattlesnake bite; the wife, of a mysterious ailment five years before. Grace had come to live with the Colemans nine years before, when she was fifteen. Luther's wife, her aunt, had died while she was away at college. Coming back for the funeral, Grace had seen her uncle's miserable loneliness, his utter inability

44

to handle any longer the details of his ambitious business; and, though he had not suggested it, she had canceled her plans to return East and stayed here ever since, an efficient housekeeper and manager, if an unwilling one.

It would not go on long: she had that much consolation. Luther Coleman was even now more dead than alive. She watched him through the open door as she kindled a fire in the stove and put the tin coffee pot on to boil. His hands were shaking so that he could hardly hold a letter. His eyes were bleary, and his face chalk-white, as if the blood had vanished from beneath. The doctor who had examined him last gave him a year at the most, vowing that no man could drink that much and live forever. Luther had a furious cough, which shook his wasted body.

She came back into the office. "A man was here to see you, a Texan."

"Did you fix him up, honey?"

"Yes. He wanted to deposit some money. Ten thousand dollars. And some kind of deed."

"Did you put it in the safe?"

"Yes."

"Good girl," Luther Coleman sighed. "I don't know what I'd do without you, honey."

She did not answer. It was obvious what he would do—nothing. Life held just that for Luther Coleman.

Grace wanted to be sorry for him. She could remember a different man, could recall his plans for the bank and the store, his appointment as postmaster, his purchase of controlling interest in the stage line between Shadrock and Mount Cloister. The latter had been trifled away. So had the business which once had made him the richest man in Shadrock, a man who profited even when cattle were cheap or dying, and to whom the proudest ranchmen in the valley,

45

even Edgar Martin and Jupiter Cross, had to come for credit. Because of those debts, he had ruled Shadrock politically long after he retired as sheriff.

His wife's death had broken him. Once, thick-tongued with liquor, eager to talk to anyone, Luther had told Grace that he was responsible for his wife's death. "I killed her as much as if I had taken a gun and shot her down," he had wailed.

But Theresa Coleman had died a natural death. A surprising death, true enough, but a natural one. One day she had been in the pink of health, sturdy and good-humored and affectionate; then she had begun to decline, and she had passed away in a blinding sandstorm when no one even knew that she was ailing.

It helped Grace to endure her uncle that he had been a strong man until then.

"I don't know why," she told Luther, "but this Texan wanted you to know about the deposit. He said to tell you that a man named Thompson sent him to you."

"Thompson!" whispered Luke. "Drifting Dan Thompson!"

"I believe he said that."

"My God!" her uncle croaked, and buried his face in his hands.

She was stunned by his manner. Not in a long time had Luther Coleman shown interest in anything; much less, dismay.

"A deed!" he whispered. Then he stood up. "Seen Ed Martin on the street in the last hour?"

"No."

"I'll mosey down to the saloon," he whispered. "Ed will want to know about this."

She barred his way. "Is that the way to run a bank?"

46

she demanded. "Should you run to Ed Martin and tell him what our customers deposit with us?"

He patted her shoulder. "You don't understand, honey," he said with a pitiful attempt at a smile. "This is something I got to tell Ed about."

"But your coffee is hot," she protested.

"I'll drink it later." Hat on, he started for the door.

At that moment Newt Norton entered.

"In a hurry, Luke?"

"Yes, Newt."

"Won't take me but a minute," shrugged the marshal. "This Texas man made a deposit today. Any objections to telling me what?"

"Money," Luther answered jerkily. "Ten thousand dollars."

"Thanks," Newt nodded. His deep eyes studied the banker somberly. "He is making talk about having known Drifting Dan Thompson down in Texas, Luke."

"Is he?" Luther asked hoarsely.

"Yes."

Newt stood aside to let Coleman pass. "I guess," murmured the marshal, "Drifting Dan didn't die in that fire after all."

Luther hurried out the door. Newt turned to Grace and tipped his hat. Then, lips tight, he wandered down the street, turning at the hotel to take a trail which led toward the river. This was one man who could wander in the direction of Ramona Custer's without being hailed from the porch by Jeanne, the little half-breed who was at present Ramona's only "girl." Not for a long time had Ramona's girls propositioned the marshal by look or speech, not even when there had been eight or ten on the madam's "string." Newt, they all knew, was Ramona's special property.

47

Grace Coleman turned into the kitchen and listlessly began to make preparations for the evening meal.

Why had her uncle lied to Newt Norton!

Newt did not stay long at Ramona's. He came back shortly along the path and got his horse from the livery stable and rode slowly toward the pass, turning off at a wide trail on the Shadrock side of Frenchman's Creek. He mounted a ridge from which he could see the Tall T wagons beneath him, and the Texas cattle spread out over the flats.

He stopped and watched a moment. Smoke drifted up from two fires; some of the hands were playing cards while others were engaged in makeshift tasks like repairing saddles and braiding hair ropes.

The grim marshal shook his head. No doubt of it, this outfit had come here on business. Talk reaching town had said there were twenty riders to two thousand stockers, which was plenty of man power, far more than the average outfit ever dreamed of carrying on a trail drive.

Newt then turned his horse toward the pine ridges, splashing across the creek higher up, and riding slowly through waving blue stem. This was winter range for the Sloping S. Ed Martin usually ran his stock higher up in good seasons, saving the grass around the creek mouth for the hot dry season when he'had sold off his culls and had to keep his stockers going until the winter rains set in and the higher ground was dotted with bunch or rescue grass.

The marshal left the creek bank and went up through the first layer of straggling pines. Smoke curled high above him; he breasted a sharp ridge and saw the Kimberlin cabin in its upland valley that was no more than eighty acres in area, and was split by a spring overflow which seeped out of the rimside in all kinds of weather.

The Kimberlins had been here when Newt Norton came

48

to Sunrise Valley; and that was a long time ago. Certainly, Newt mused, no nester had ever found a more desirable spot. In Bill Bradley's tenure at the Sloping S, Calvin Kimberlin had gone his way unmolested, for no more than a handful of cattle could graze this valley, and its inacessibility at roundup time had made it a lost useless cove. In the twenty-five years since that, the Kimberlins had had a precarious existence, for Ed Martin was another type of man. Yet, except for tongue lashings and bullyings, he had not bothered them; and here was their cabin that had been thrown up more than a score of years ago, with little addition and no improvements.

Calvin left the pines and came out to meet the marshal. He was a tall gaunt man, peak-thin as if his had been a one-sided battle against starvation.

"Howdy, marshal. Set awhile."

Maude lumbered out of the cabin, and then Katie, her eyes dark sullen pools. Newt gave the girl a fleeting study. There would be trouble here if there wasn't already. Valley talk said the girl was more like Calvin Kimberlin, shiftless and pouty. Maude Kimberlin, who had brought at least half of the valley children into the world in her role as a midwife, was respected by her neighbors, though hers was such a rasping, driving nature that genuine liking was impossible.

Norton rolled off his horse.

"Maw, can we serve the marshal some coffee?" asked Calvin. "And mebbe he'll stay for supper."

"Coffee, yes," nodded Newt. "No supper, thanks. I gotta ride back."

"Sure," said Maude. "Set the pot on, Katie."

The girl moved to obey, but without alacrity. The thin cotton dress she was wearing did not conceal the fullness of her hips and breasts. Newt Norton sighed. No wonder the boys gibed Cherry Carr in the town saloon about the nester's daughter.

"I reckon," Newt said, "that you know about the trail herd. And this Texan who doesn't wear a gun."

"Heard some talk," Maude admitted.

Newt knew enough to address his remarks to her. Calvin, in her presence, was a completely dominated man; but no one blamed Maude for that, not even in a country where men were supposed to "wear the pants." There had been no alternative to her taking the reins.

Newt studied her face. Perhaps he was closer to actually liking Maude than anyone in the valley. But that could be said about Newt Norton and almost any family which lived in the shadow of the high steep pass. Not in over twenty years had he been compelled to draw his gun on a man; and his job as marshal had not put him at outs with any of them. He did not bear a grudge because he had twice been defeated for sheriff, and many people who were outwardly friendly with him had obviously voted against him. He knew why they had turned him down, and he did not blame them.

"It has been a long time since the Bradley fire," Newt said slowly. Now Katie had brought his coffee, without cream, and he rolled it around and around in his cup in lieu of using a spoon, but without spilling a drop. "Some of the details, I never did get straight. It wasn't my job, as I was just a marshal. Reckon you know more about that fire, Maude, than anybody in the valley."

Her face blazed with sudden anger. "Reckon I did," she sniffed. "And if I'd been a man I would have shot down Luke Coleman and Ed Martin on sight. I ain't ever forgiven you for not doing it yourself, Newt Norton."

"At times I hold the same grudge against myself," he admitted. "But the law I stood for didn't reach out that far."

"Seems like," Maude said grimly, "the law you stand for never reaches as far as the weak, Newt."

There was more than passing bitterness in her observation. Newt nodded. His kind of law had never reached out to protect her and her kind of people. And never would, in this country.

"Reckon it's got its limits," he admitted gruffly. Sometimes a law man wished that he wrote the laws as well as carried them out. Sometimes a man got as weary of what a star stood for as the people to whom that star represented a narrowness that frequently reached the point of injustice. "The talk was, Maude, that Theresa Bradley was in your cabin with her young uns. Is that right?"

"I ain't ever said yes and I ain't ever said no," Maude Kimberlin said harshly. "It ain't my place to speak up alone against Ed Martin and his kind. This valley let it ride, and I ain't noticed a spark of interest since then. Why should I talk now? So you could go back to town and start trouble over again after all these years and Ed Martin would come riding to settle with me for my blabbing tongue. No, Newt Norton. I ain't saying what happened that night. I would have told a jury then, even if it had meant my life. I might even tell a jury now. But nobody around this valley has the guts to throw such a charge in Ed Martin's face. The Mahoneys and that danged Jupiter Cross got what they wanted—they got rid of a man who could outtrade 'em, and who would have swallowed 'em up in due time. Luke Coleman got what he wanted, 'cept he didn't have the gumption to hang on to it. And you—Newt, I never knew what you wanted."

"Nor I," he nodded. "Bill Bradley was my friend, and Drifting Dan—my side-kick."

"Was he really?" Maude asked curiously. "Even after that gun fight?"

"Never until then. Men like Dan had a code. They got to keep going until somebody gets the best of 'em. Dan was tickled pink that I winged him. He was a partner."

Newt waited a minute. Then, studying Maude's face with his grave eyes: "This Texan, this Brad Hunter, is spreading talk that he ran into Dan down in Texas. It would make me feel a lot better to know he got clear, Maude."

Maude sat with tight lips. Apparently her mind was unchanged about keeping what she knew under her hat.

"This Texan is coming geared for trouble," went on Newt. "He's a queer galoot. Ed Martin sung him out, and the Texan backed down. Don't even pack a gun. But he has bedded his cows down in Martin's best grass, and he has enough men with him to shoot up this country from hell to breakfast. He broadcasts that the mouth of Frenchman's Creek is public land in the first place, and that Ed Martin hasn't got a deed to the Sloping S in the second."

"The talk I heard," Maude nodded, "ran like that."

"There were two Bradley kids. The story goes that they came down here and caught scarlet fever; that your little boy died, too. You came to town, and I stood good for two caskets. Remember that?"

"You got your money back," Maude snapped, suddenly red-faced and trembling. "People in this valley raised more than enough."

"Oh, sure, it never cost me a cent. Wouldn't have mattered if it had. But weren't there some rumors about Drifting Dan Thompson getting away?"

"I heard 'em," Maude admitted. "Me, I don't know. I never had much truck with Drifting Dan."

"There were three kids," Newt mused. "You bought two

52

caskets, Maude. Mebbe the other one didn't die. Mebbe Dan Thompson didn't, either." He sighed. "I rode out to the Bradley place a couple of days later. The house was burned plumb to the ground. There was no way of knowing whether Dan got away or not. The Martin gang said they winged him. The Cross riders said they saw him fall. Bill Bradley was dead, we know. But Bill's wife and her two kids got away without being hurt. Jupiter's men made the Martin gang stop shooting until they were clear. Everybody knows that."

"They got here," Maude agreed. "They came running in like the devil was behind 'em. Which it was—Ed Martin. The baby wasn't over two weeks old, and as sick as its mother. Poor Mrs. Bradley didn't have a chance to live. She saw her husband drop. Mebbe she would have died anyhow, but that sure helped."

"I know," Newt said gently. "But did the Bradley button die, Maude? Here is this young Texan talking glibly about knowing Drifting Dan Thompson. Walks right into the bank and asks for Luke Coleman. Leaves a mysterious deed there and ten thousand bucks in cash. Ain't this Brad Hunter the son of Bill Bradley come back to Sunrise Pass to settle for a crime which happened twenty-five years ago?"

"All I know," Maude answered doggedly, "is what I've told you. Don't drag me into any of your talk, Newt Norton. I ain't saying any more."

She jumped up. "It ain't healthy. Cal and me just got a few more years. We want to spend them here, where we're used to things."

Newt nodded. He couldn't demand any more. For what could his law do against Ed Martin's swift and terrible retribution!

Chapter Five

GRACE WAITED a half-hour for her uncle to return, then ate alone. It was only one of many lonely meals, but tonight she resented Luther's absence more than ever. She asked herself for the millionth time why she should stay here and look after the waning years and the failing business of a man who so obviously cared nothing about either. He had gone in search of Ed Martin, but she knew where he had ended up. By now he might even be in Ramona's. She could forgive him his drinking more easily than she could his periodical visits to the unpainted frame house down the path which no Shadrock girl or matron ever dared walk.

She washed the dishes slowly. A cake she had baked that morning lay untouched, and there was only a small slab missing out of two apple pies. Both represented so much wasted effort; Luther would probably never touch either. He couldn't last long, for he wasn't eating enough to keep a bird alive and, as Dr. Dorris pointed out, no man could live on whisky alone.

She brushed the frayed edges of her curls and sat on the small covered porch which fronted the side street—or path, for no wagon and team ever turned here. The loneliness she had been able to curb before rushed up at her with a savage surging force; she recalled seeing the Atlantic Ocean while in the East, and compared her feelings with that relentless tide. Luther Coleman must die soon, for she couldn't endure living in this isolated town much longer.

Twilight came slipping around the corner, soothing and gentle in its coloring, but discomforting indeed to a lonely girl wrapped in thought and bitter self-pity. She heard the clump of boots on the board walk in front of the store and told herself quickly that she wouldn't open the door for any man in Shadrock. She had. nothing else to do, but she wouldn't admit anyone.

Then the bootsteps came closer, and Brad Hunter turned the corner with the squint-eyed man at his heels. They stood together talking in low tones, and she saw Brad point to the deserted blacksmith's shop across the path. Behind its crumbling timbers grew a grove of mesquites; and the two men tramped over and through the deserted back lot where for years now Shadrock had dumped its refuse. Then they came back to the corner.

Grace Coleman with sudden daring opened the gate and called to them:

"Evening, Texas."

They turned, and their startled expressions showed that seeing her was the last thing they had expected. Their confusion piqued her a little; the thought had first come to her, and had swelled into a hope, that perhaps Brad Hunter wanted to see her again, and was roving this sidewalk in that expectation.

"Evening, Miss Coleman," he said politely.

"Looking over our town?"

"Sorta."

"There aren't many points of interest," she shrugged. "Men from Texas must have seen this kind of town until they are sick of it."

"Reckon it's our kind of town," Squint said. "We were just saying that it makes us homesick."

Her speech was addressed to both of them, but her eyes

were upon Brad Hunter with a strange defiant regard for what was conventional, and what she had always represented before.

"It's a lonely little town," she murmured.

She was wearing a cool white dress, with an artificial flower in her hair. She had not known why she had taken the trouble to dress; now she knew, and her self-reproach brought new color to her cheeks that Brad Hunter could see in the pale flickering light.

"Reckon a woman like you," twinkled Squint, "never is very lonely. At least you wouldn't be back in Texas. Would have so many waddies hanging around that the calves would have to come in of their own accord to get branded."

Brad chuckled. "Squint is the sweet-talking one, ain't he? Got more gals on the trail than any other four Texas men."

"And you, Mr. Hunter," she questioned calmly, "how many have you?"

"None to speak of—right now," he grinned.

She hesitated. They were being polite, yes. But any man would be polite under such circumstances. How far did she dare to go?

"If you'd care to come in on the porch," she proposed, "I'd serve you hungry Texas men some coffee and pie."

"Pie!" gasped Squint. "Did you say 'pie'?"

"I did," she smiled.

Grace Coleman served pie and coffee, secretly giving thanks for the hunch which had set her to baking that morning. The two men chattered of the trail and their first impressions of this country. They had a humor she had not noticed in Wyoming men, and yet that same quaint reserve she had observed in all western men. Having been East, she had a medium of comparison.

Squint excused himself after his second piece of pie.

"Think there might be some of our boys down at the saloon," he murmured. "I'd better see about 'em, Brad."

"I'll go with you," Hunter proposed.

"No call for you to leave," Squint urged, a twinkle in his eyes. "I'll mosey down, and if everything is quiet I'll be right back."

Brad Hunter agreed; but it was plain to her that the Tall T owner was uncomfortable. The way he squirmed and kept looking at his watch brought an angry flash to her blue eyes. Finally she said:

"I think you'd be happier if you joined your foreman at the saloon, Mr. Hunter."

There was frost in her voice; he shivered before it.

"I'm sorry," he said in a low voice. "I have something on my mind, and I know I'm bad company. Mebbe I can come back—again."

"You can," she said, a relieved smile breaking across her face. "I'm sitting here every night about this time. You'll be welcome."

"Good," he nodded.

"I enjoyed your visit," she told him gravely.

She had. Shadrock, where the most routine action was brought to the attention of all, and became a topic of general conversation, would say that she was throwing her loop at the lean young man from Texas who had come driving a trail herd over Sunrise Pass. Probably even now tongues were clucking, for it had worried most of Shadrock's adult population for a long time that such an eligible girl stayed single. Most credited her responsibility for Luther Coleman with her steadfast refusal to take any suitor seriously, and pitied her for it. She did not deny this interpretation; but she had known even before Brad Hunter's coming that it wasn't so.

57

At first she had felt it a duty to do what she could for the uncle who had taken her into his home as his own daughter; but that had been a long time ago. She would leave at a moment's notice, and Luther Coleman could lie in the bed he had made for himself with his drinking and his exaggerated fears of Ed Martin.

Yes, she was throwing a loop. Why not? The pass had turned everybody back—except Brad Hunter.

"You must come again," she murmured, walking with him to the gate. Her tone was an insistence rather than an invitation.

Brad Hunter looked down at her with a tightening of his lips. By day she was neat-looking and efficient, the kind of woman a man needed to supplement the awful details of life which a man never seems able to master. By night she was a beckoning far-off mystery, with a gleam in her eyes that set a man's blood a-tingling. He was human. He was also young, and he knew what loneliness meant—knew more about it than Grace Coleman, who was pitying herself, could ever imagine. For he had been raised without father or mother, with no other guiding hand than a limping half-blind gunslick who had fled one range in fear of his life.

But Brad Hunter had a self-control that Grace Coleman lacked, and he used it. Ordinarily it is a woman's duty to hold back, a man's to storm ahead. It was not a lack of recklessness which kept Brad's arms at his side. His was a philosophy typical of his country and his time—to ride every trail to its end, sometimes unthinking, always without regrets.

But this was a possibility closed to him even before he had sighted it—closed to him by circumstances which Grace Coleman at the moment knew nothing about. And which, if she had known, would have made little difference.

To her invitation that he come again he murmured, "I would like that," lifted his hat, and walked away.

She looked after him for long moments, leaning her weight on the gatepost. There was a tune on her lips as well as a smile, and Newt Norton, who always seemed to be everywhere, seeing everything, bobbed his head in approval of her sudden change of mood. Nothing of his friendly solicitation ever showed in his somber face, but it was always there; after twenty-six years as marshal of a town which dwindled in population every year, with no newcomers except for transient riders who didn't matter, a man learned a lot about the people of a town, especially a man like Newt Norton who in his queer way liked people for what they were, and understood them far better than they would ever give him credit for doing.

Norton lifted his hat as he passed the corner, turned, and resumed his walk down the dusty street now shimmering from the first adventurous streaks of moonlight breaking over the pass. In front of Fatty's Bar he saw Brad Hunter join Squint Elliott, with three Texas riders in the background; and he wondered why they did not go on into the saloon. Then a swirl of light silver-gray dust brought Ed Martin and Cherry Carr galloping into Shadrock, with no fewer than four Sloping S hands gleefully hailing the oil lantern above Fatty's door; and Newt quickened his steps.

But there was no trouble. The Sloping S men did not seem to notice the five Texans who sat on their haunches near their horses, rolling smokes and completely absorbed in their own talk. Brad Hunter said, "Evening, marshal," as Newt paced up, and he answered curtly.

The marshal didn't like this queer peace. He knew this

59

country and its people, their quick flashing tempers, their sullen feuds, their dogged pursuit of a trail that might lead off into nowhere. Range wars had started over less than this, and Newt couldn't understand why this one didn't launch a feud immediately. Yet right past the Texans had stalked Ed Martin and his men, without a hint of a challenge; and the Texans whose leader didn't pack a gun did not seize the opportunity to beat a hasty retreat, but held their ground as if the Sloping S men inside did not matter at all, and only their small personal talk was important.

Inside, Ed Martin was buying a round for the crowd, which happened seldom. He leaned against the bar with his weight on his elbow, and his dark eyes were glowering at the door as the marshal came in. Yet he did not see Norton, and the law man knew that this glare was for the Texans loitering outside. The Sloping S men took their glasses and sat at a battered card table, but not to play poker. Seeing their heads close together, and Martin's lips moving rapidly, Newt guessed that their attention was bent on a grimmer game than poker. He nodded to Fatty and touched his lips gingerly to the hot liquor. He was not much of a drinking man, and what drinks he did down were usually at Ramona's in the shelter of her private room.

But Newt Norton was also gripped in the wave of restlessness which had swept Shadrock ever since this trail herd had come over Sunrise Pass and Brad Hunter had ridden his sleek roan into town. He tried to shut out the casual drifting sounds to hear what was being discussed at the table. All he heard was a quick retort from Cherry Carr to something Ed Martin was saying.

"I'll be damned if I will, Ed," snapped the redhead. "That ain't in my contract."

Newt was under no illusions as to the character of the

men who rode for the Sloping S. He was well aware that gunfire might break out any time between Ed Martin's men and Jupiter Cross's riders. Jupiter and Ed took deliberate pains never to meet in Shadrock because of a clash over spring roundup three seasons before. Jupiter claimed that Ed's boys had slapped an iron on every stray they saw, without making any effort to settle the ownership of the maverick. Most men in the valley believed Jupiter's story. Jupiter had come to the sheriff with his complaint, but Sam Dugan was a mild man and let the troublesome matter drop. Newt had not been concerned. He was marshal, not sheriff: his job was to keep order in a Wyoming town that had been listless and even stagnant for a long time, and his two offers to assume greater responsibilities had been turned down. Indications were, however, that he might start earning his pay any moment.

There was a scraping of chairs behind him. His eyes leaped to the plate-glass mirror above the bar. Cherry Carr was walking away from the table with a swagger, and one of the riders known as Hogshead Turpin was coming with him, leaving three men to sit with Ed Martin. The ranchman glared after Cherry with unmistakable resentment, then shrugged his shoulders and poured out another drink around and talked faster and lower.

Cherry came to the bar and gave the marshal a nod. Newt's curiosity was not satisfied with that.

"I'll buy a drink," the officer said pleasantly.

Cherry lifted his eyebrows. Newt didn't usually make such offers, or accept them.

"Bueno," he nodded. "Mebbe my friends will see me. Do my reputation good to be on such friendly terms with the law."

Norton sized him up with a sidewise look. Cherry wasn't

61

happy. The marshal knew the redhead's type. Perhaps Cherry was the fastest man in Wyoming with a six-gun. Talk put it so. Talk even stated that Carr was faster than Newt Norton had ever been, even in the marshal's younger days when he had winged Drifting Dan Thompson, and won a reputation that had spread all over the West. Newt didn't care to make a test.

Probably Cherry was the best of the Sloping S crew. He had his faults—many of them. Norton didn't like what he had heard about Cherry's treatment of women; but a rider like Cherry had his code, and wouldn't vary from it. Some things he would do, and to hell with society that thought he was breaking a law. But some things he wouldn't. Perhaps this proved he had a conscience. Cherry wouldn't have said so. Newt sighed. All that was wrong with young men like Cherry was the way they had been raised. Certainly the redhead was careless with a branding iron; that was his reputation, and that was why better outfits than the Sloping S didn't want him. But probably, except where branding irons and women were concerned, Cherry was an honest man. He had killed men, and wasn't above provoking a quarrel just to impress standers-by with his speed and accuracy. But that was his heritage, to hold life cheaply, even his own.

What had Ed Martin wanted Cherry to do that had angered the flame-haired man, that had sent Carr stalking away from the table in disgust? Norton wondered about this as he lifted his glass in a quick gesture to Cherry and Hogshead Turpin, and drained it at a gulp. Yes, there were things Cherry wouldn't do—such as bushwhack a man. Cherry might walk into any man's gun, including Norton's. But he wouldn't shoot a man in his back. Newt would never be afraid to turn his back on Cherry.

Now Cherry strolled outside. Newt turned for another look at the table. Ed Martin was still talking, a gleam in his black eyes. One of his three listeners was named Duval; the boys called him Jinx. Norton had spent a lifetime sizing up men, and he was seldom wrong. Whatever the job was, he mused, Martin would probably pick Duval to do it. With perhaps Skinny Ryan, the shifty-eyed pock-marked bronc' peeler, to help out. Ryan could have worked for a dozen spreads once, but whispers had spread around about him. He was a crack hand with bronc's, but none of the better outfits would touch him with a ten-foot pole because of his reputation. Norton didn't know what was wrong with Skinny; the rumors didn't go that far.

The marshal went outside. Brad Hunter and the Tall T men were still swapping talk about themselves.

"Sit down, marshal," invited Brad. "We're cussing this Wyoming country up and down the river."

"After the trouble you went to, to get here," Newt said dryly, "you oughta like it."

"Dan Thompson was getting old when I knew him," grinned Brad. "He talked about rich grass and cool breezes and clear water. He must have been out of his head to send me up here."

"Thompson sent you up here?" demanded Newt, his voice sharp and his body tense. He had guessed as much, but this was the first time Brad Hunter had said so.

"Didn't you know that?" the Texan countered.

Newt jerked a hand back toward the saloon. "Does Martin know that?"

"I've told enough people," grinned Brad. "The word ought to have got to him by now."

"What did Thompson tell you about this Wyoming country? Did he mention the Sloping S?"

"Some."

Newt Norton sighed. "That was a long time ago," he said slowly. "It's dust on the trail. Some people think it's a good idea not to stir up too much dust, Hunter."

"Down Texas way," murmured Brad, "we got used to dust."

Newt hesitated, groping for words. Now he knew who this lean young man was. He wanted to ask a hundred questions—if Drifting Dan was still alive, if Brad knew the full particulars about the murder of his father and the death of his mother. And the mysterious deed left for deposit at Luther Coleman's bank with such a fanfare! If this Brad Hunter was indeed the son of Bill Bradley, and did actually possess a deed to the Sloping S ranch, then why enter Sunrise Valley under another name, and why delay? Ed Martin was tough, and the Sloping S men would probably put up a fight, particularly Cherry Carr; but if the law was unquestionably on the Texan's side his rider could be deputized at a wave of Newt Norton's hand, and they could handle the Sloping S crew!

Now Cherry Carr came back by the saloon. The redhead stopped, the tip of his cigarette no more of a flame than his hair, and there was an amused challenge in his drawl.

"You Texas men sure take up a lot of room."

Again Newt wondered what Martin had wanted Cherry to do. Certainly it must be tied up with this Brad Hunter, and these Texas men. Cherry had walked away from Ed's scheming, yet here he was giving the Texans an opening if they wanted it. It wasn't the fight, then, that Cherry had turned down; it was the way of fighting.

"In case there ain't room for you to get by, Red," Brad Hunter said meekly, "we'll be glad to move."

Cherry glared down at the squatting Texan. The suspicion was in his mind, as it was in Norton's, that the Texan might be making fun of him. He stepped forward suddenly, and his knee gave the man a gentle shove.

"Men who don't pack hardware shouldn't take up so much of the sidewalk," he jeered. "Up here in Wyoming we reserve our sidewalks for men."

Brad Hunter steadied himself with his hand to keep from falling. There was a murmur from his four companions, but he held up his hand and the noise ceased.

"Next time, Cherry," he said softly, "I'll see that you have enough room."

The redhead didn't like this answer. It was his creed that this kind of talk never settled anything. Nesters shrank from cowmen, but not a young man who owned an outfit such as the Tall T, who bossed a crew of twenty men and apparently held their respect and allegiance. Newt wondered how Brad Hunter could possibly take this.

Cherry waited a moment; then, when the Texans had nothing else to say, moved on with a low chuckle. He swung into his saddle and was off at a gallop. A rider like Cherry was hard on his horses. None of them could run fast enough to suit him.

Norton saw Brad's face, hard and lean and lips tight, and shook his head. There would be something between these two—Cherry Carr and Brad Hunter. The chip on Cherry's shoulder would always be there. And, sooner or later, one of these Texas men would make a pass at it.

The marshal also walked on. Some of the drinkers at Fatty's were leaving. There was a clatter of hoofbeats behind Newt as he walked toward Ramona's for his nightly drink and visit with the woman who had held his interest a long, long time. An hour later he came back by the saloon and saw that the Texans had moved across the street into the shadows. He could see their cigarette tips glowing and hear their low talk. Ed Martin and his men had left.

Newt walked by the Coleman building. The porch was deserted, and the house was dark. He saw a figure stumbling along the walk when he turned.

"I'll give you a hand, Luke," he said curtly.

And he helped the half-drunken faltering man toward Fatty's, where Fatty himself took him in charge and led him into a small private room where, Newt knew, he drank himself insensible more often than not. Sometimes it was noon before a sympathetic soul aroused Coleman and sent him home.

"Good old Newt," murmured Luther. "Best damn marshal west of Abilene."

Newt Norton's lips quirked in disgust. Once he had actually sought provocation to shoot this man down. But then Luther Coleman had been a physical giant, a man new to Wyoming, a trader who had pulled heavy wagons behind him from the East and had made money in booming Shadrock from the start. He had even been a good sheriff for a while. Then the mining interests had pulled out and his bank and store had lost trade and, in desperation, he had turned to a deal with Ed Martin that still made Newt burn whenever he thought of it. For that he would have cheerfully killed Luke Coleman—twenty-five years ago. Now he felt only disgust for the man who had degenerated into a cheap drunkard, who raided his own cash drawer to buy whisky, and who held on in business only because he had the good sense to stay out of his store and bank and leave his niece to greet customers.

Now the street was deserted except for the Texans in the shadows. Newt turned into the hotel, unstrapping his

66

gun as he walked up the rickety stairs. Perhaps his was the jitteriness of old age. Perhaps he was never again to earn his marshal's pay in dying Shadrock.

Cherry, riding with his usual haste, reached the Kimberlin clearing just as the final shivers of daylight were backing up across the pass heights, snarling in defiance at the onrushing banks of darkness closing in on all sides. The three Kimberlins were sitting on their uncovered porch, Calvin usurping the rocking chair and Katie sitting on the steps, her gingham skirt pulled tight around her knees.

Cherry dismounted with a grin for the disapproving glare from Maude Kimberlin.

"Gonna make a quick look around the valley for strays," he announced. "Won't bother you none."

"At night?" Maude asked crossly.

"Camping out," Cherry nodded. "Come over to get an early start."

"Hmph!" snorted Maude, who did not believe a word of it.

Calvin tried to engage the Sloping S foreman in talk, but Cherry answered only in monosyllables. Talking to Cal Kimberlin was not his idea of spending a pleasant evening.

The moon came over the pass in one reckless leap, and Cherry motioned toward it.

"Purty moon, ain't it?" he asked.

He was looking at Cal, but his words were meant for Katie. He shot her a sidewise glance, and knew she had caught his meaning.

Now he slouched toward his horse. He had made his gesture, and he was confident as to the results. This chubby-cheeked girl would slip out of the house as soon as she could. He could tell by the toss of her black head and her quietness. Right now, she hadn't made up her mind. She was still wrestling with her decision.

He rode up the valley, even mounting the slopes. Then, by the spring mouth, a hundred yards from the Kimberlin cabin, he spread his bedroll and built a small fire. There was no necessity of either, for he did not intend to spend the night here. But Katie must have something to guide her through the darkness.

Would she come? As Cherry smoked, he deliberated with a grin curving his lips. Of course she would come. His way of treating women nearly always worked with nester girls. And sometimes with the wives. It was his sheer audacity as well as his good looks. He hurled a challenge into their faces, and they couldn't resist it. Their vanity wouldn't let them. They had to see if they held the same attraction for Cherry Carr that other women did.

He was right. He had stretched out on his blanket and was dozing when he heard shy furtive footsteps. Instantly he sat up.

"Over here, Katie," he called.

He was dozing away from the fire. After all, it was still July and the breeze that stirred the hidden valley did no more than whet a man's appetite for coolness.

She came slowly toward him, and he saw by the flickering moonlight that she was a little frightened, that she was coming toward him with unwilling steps.

"Knew you'd take pity on a lonesome man," he chuckled, now standing up. "Besides, it's too purty a night to waste sitting inside a house."

She nodded, mute, frozen. He reached out and caught her hand.

"Let's mosey up toward the spring," he proposed.

Catherine Kimberlin offered no protest.

Once he stopped and studied her. The moonlight showed up the high full coloring of her face.

"You're sweet," he muttered, and caught her to him roughly.

The night's tinting had done wonders with her. That and her nearness. But, even while he ground his lips against hers, Cherry Carr was laughing at himself. Every woman did that to him in the moonlight.

He released her as suddenly as he had caught her in his arms.

"Let's go on," he said huskily.

Katie Kimberlin stepped away from him. "No," she whispered, holding her hand to her lips.

"Yes," he insisted, and put his arm around her.

Her feet wouldn't move until he exerted pressure against her. Then she followed, each step a stubborn one, each step a lagging one.

And the grin on Cherry Carr's face broadened!

Chapter Six

GRACE COLEMAN HEARD the noise from a long distance, a confused sound creeping through tiers of heavy sleep. She awoke in stages, at first drowsily turning and tossing, attaching no importance to the faint sounds, feeling only irritation that her slumber had been disturbed. Then, in sudden horror, it dawned upon her that the sound was that of an explosion, and very near.

At first she thought it might have been a celebrating cowboy firing off his revolver just outside the canvas-curtained porch where she slept, the coolest part of the house during these July nights. And yet—it was different from a gunshot. As she waited, half afraid and half amused at her own concern, the booming sound was followed by a scraping of feet, and she could place the noise.

Someone was in the bank! And that explosion had been the burglar blowing open the safe!

She pulled on her kimono and crept noiselessly to the door. There were still sounds coming through the wall, and she was conscious of her own trembling, and then a feeling of indignation that Luther Coleman was not there to protect his own.

Moonlight streamed in from the open windows, and by its glow she found uncle's shotgun, which was the only weapon in the house. Its barrel clanged as she took it off the deer antlers which supported it, and she caught her breath lest the marauder had heard, and been warned. No, there was still the scraping. Whoever it was, was a clumsy burglar. She stole forward, fumbling with the shotgun's catch, wishing she knew more about guns. As a girl she had tried to kill jack rabbits and doves, but without success. She recalled that it was this selfsame shotgun she had fired, and that its safety had to be pulled back. The clicking to her was a sound that should have awakened the dead. But still the burglar worked on, and she reached the door and caught its knob and shuddered.

Did she dare open it! Why wasn't Uncle Luke here to do such things! The wiser course would be to scream; perhaps that would frighten the burglar away. But no. Other women in this country had fired off guns in protection of their homes. Her own mother had held her own in a fight with Sioux Indians.

Holding the gun high, until it interfered with her movements, she turned the door knob, hoping against hope that it wouldn't squeak. She was afraid. To throw open that door might mean a gunshot tearing in her direction. But she had it to do.

The gun barrel clanged against the door sill, and she knew from the sudden silence that the intruder had heard her, and that he was waiting in the darkness for her to open the door.

Panic seized her. She could *not* open that door. Then, gritting her teeth until the marauder must have heard that noise too, she slid back along the wall, holding the door ajar with her hand. She pushed the gun barrel into the space and was grateful for the squeak of the hinges and the rasping sound as the door rubbed against the sill.

A blue flashing flame and a heavy roar sent her crouching against the wall. The bullet tore through the half-opened door not two feet from her. Breathlessly she waited.

What if there were other shots! These were thin wooden walls; bullets could tear right through, riddling her as she crouched tense and frightened.

But, instead, she heard more rustling, and then furtive footsteps across the building, the creak of the gate opening, and then someone fumbling with the latch on the front door. She did not wonder that the burglar was able to break the lock from the outside; it was old and rusty, unchanged and unoiled in long years.

She thrust the gun around the door sill and fired, falling to her knees more from the sheer weakness of her legs than from intent to shoot low. She heard spattering sounds and knew that her buckshot had crashed into the wooden partition separating the bank from the store shelves. There was at least one clang as a shot hit iron.

Now the front door was open, and for a fleeting second she saw a bent dark shape. It was a quick but perfect target, but Grace Coleman could not get her shotgun up in time. Then she saw through the plate-glass windows that a shadow was flitting around the side of the building, and she sensed that the burglar had tethered his horse on the side street.

Much of her fright left her. She darted back through the canvased porch and flung open the door opening out of their residence quarters. There was a furtive shape across the street and she threw the shotgun to her shoulder and fired.

The gun had not kicked before—or else she hadn't noticed it. Now it knocked her flat with its repercussion, bringing swift burning pain to her shoulder. As she scrambled up she heard the sharp clatter of a horse breaking into a gallop and a man's loud "Damn."

And the clump of high-heeled boots turning the corner of the bank.

"What's up?" she heard a voice shout. Then, even louder: "Squint, where are you?"

It was Brad Hunter. Grace Coleman was suddenly wavering on her feet.

"Mr. Hunter," she called out. "Please help me—Mr. Hunter."

Now he saw her by the gate and ran to her. The touch of his hand on her arm inspired her to stand erect, and to even give him a faint smile.

"Someone—robbed the bank," she panted. "I shot at him—out there." She pointed toward the shadows behind the deserted blacksmith's shop. There she had seen the flitting shape. "The gun kicked me. I'm all right."

Brad released her with a "Damn!" of his own and ran across the path.

"Squint, where are you?" he called again.

His answer came from the bushes, weak. "Got me, podner. Right here."

The Texan found his riding boss lying across a mesquite stump, hanging to its gnarled support.

"Got me in the leg," Squint panted. "Dunno how it happened. I was watching the guy through the window like you said to. He ducked this way, and I hit for the dirt *muy pronto*. Something hit from behind."

"It was Miss Coleman," Brad murmured. "She thought you were the burglar."

Squint suddenly thought of something as he took Brad's arm and pulled up. "I can walk a little this way," he said through tight lips. "Just the leg, that's all. But, podner, how in hell am I gonna prove I *ain't* a burglar!"

Brad lit a match and saw blood seeping down Squint's trouser legs. He tore at the cloth and sighed.

"You got enough buckshot in you to turn you black," he growled.

Now there were more footsteps. Newt Norton puffed around the corner, his gun out, his trousers pulled on over his underwear, his feet sockless in his high-heeled boots.

"What happened?" panted the marshal.

Before Grace had finished explaining, the marshal came across the street and gave Brad a hand with the wounded man.

"One of your boys, huh?" he grunted.

Brad Hunter shivered. "My foreman," he agreed. Then, weakly: "But he didn't loot the bank, marshal. We were just—watching."

"Not every day," Newt said with unusual sarcasm, "a man gets to watch a bank being robbed. How bad is he hit?"

"Leg torn up pretty bad. I'll help him along, and you get a doctor."

"Oh, it's your friend!" Grace exclaimed, now crossing the street. "Take him into my house. I must have hit the wrong man."

"Mebbe," Newt grunted.

"Yes, Miss Coleman," Brad assured her. There were beads of perspiration all over the Texan's face. "The real burglar had his horse hidden back of the house."

Newt and Brad now picked up the moaning Squint and carried him into the house. Grace hurriedly lit a lamp and pointed to her own bed. Squint was laid down with haste rather than gentleness, and Newt Norton examined the leg for himself.

"He'll live," he grunted. "A little lower, though, and it would have blown out his brains."

"Sure," said Squint with a grin. "A game leg never hurt anybody. Always let a hoss do the walking anyhow."

"Shall I go for a doctor?" Grace asked.

"Please," Brad answered immediately.

Newt was bathing the wounded leg with water from the tin bucket outside the door.

"Put some of that on to boil," he grunted, waving at the bucket. "Cold water is no good at stopping an infection."

"Any chance of that?" Brad asked gravely.

"Always a chance."

Grace found Dr. Dorris already dressing. Although it was past midnight, the crashing shots had roused Shadrock from its slumber, and already half the town was well aware that a burglar had broken into Luke Coleman's bank, and that one of the Texas men had been shot. The story was out that a gang of the Texans had broken into the bank and made off with all the money on deposit. On the way back with the physician Grace was hailed twice by sleepy-eyed but interested men, but did not wait to explain.

The doctor was a scrawny little man with stiff white whiskers that gave him an owlish appearance. He gave Squint's wounds a quick study and then clucked disapprovingly.

"You won't rob any more banks for a few days, fella."

"This man didn't rob the bank," Brad put in. "The guy who did got away on a bay pony."

"And what was he doing?" demanded the physician, pointing to his patient.

Squint watched the doctor with a crooked grin. "Did you ever see a sawbones who didn't ask questions?" he demanded.

"Hmph," snorted the doctor. "Any sass out of you, young fella, and I'll agree to Newt here locking you up."

"I don't think," Brad said grimly, "there is any call for that." He turned to Grace. "Miss Coleman, my friend here wasn't trying to rob your bank."

75

She answered on a quick impulse, more impish than suspicious. "How did you know the bank was robbed?"

Brad's face reddened. He turned and winced at Newt Norton's questioning gaze. There was a twinkle in the marshal's eyes, deep back, but as usual this was hidden by his sober impassiveness.

"Come outside, Hunter," said the law man. "We'll talk this over. Miss Grace, go through the bank and see what's missing."

"Yes, of course."

Out on the porch Newt dispersed several curious citizens with "It's all right" and then shook his head slowly to Brad's quick demand:

"You don't think either Squint or me had anything to do with robbing the bank, do you?"

"I don't think so. But this is plumb funny, Hunter. You say your man was cooling his heels across the street and saw the burglar come out of the bank? Is that the way you Texans spend your time—hiding in mesquites behind deserted blacksmith shops?"

"Our horses were tethered there," Brad said. "We were going to get them. Squint was a mite ahead of me. Waiting for me there."

"What's wrong with the hitching rack down in front of the saloon?"

"My mare and Squint's mount are having an affair," Brad grinned. "They like to be off by themselves."

Newt gave him a glare. He had no liking for levity. "We'll go back inside and see what the damage is," he proposed curtly.

In the bank Grace Coleman had completed a hurried examination. The lock had been blown off the battered iron safe, and the contents rifled. But she could find only one thing missing—the package containing Brad Hunter's ten thousand dollars and the important deed he had laid so much emphasis upon.

"Nothing else," she said. "Not even the four thousand dollars we had on hand to meet Sledge Mahoney's pay roll."

Newt looked to Brad Hunter, and his deep eyes glimmered in quick amusement.

"Looks like, Hunter, your boys would try to stop burglars getting away with your own dough?"

"We only saw him for a minute," shrugged Brad. "I was across the street. Squint was behind the blacksmith's shop. Anyhow, marshal, that oughta clear us. We wouldn't break into the bank and blow up the safe to steal our dough. And deed."

"What is the deed?" Newt asked.

"I ain't saying, for a while," Brad smiled. "About the money. The bills were carefully marked, marshal. Had my brand etched in red ink in the corner. All of 'em hundreds. Identifying 'em should be pretty simple."

"Yeah," muttered Newt. "I guess so."

His glance raked Brad's face again. "Plumb clever of you," he murmured, "to have the bills marked. Your foreman saw the man. Any description of him."

"I got an idea," Brad murmured, "which outfit he came from. Want to hear it?"

"No," Newt Norton snapped. His lips tightened. "The law ain't to be used like pawns on a chessboard, Hunter. Keep your ideas to yourself. I'll handle this my own way."

"Sure, sure. Just trying to help out."

Norton stalked back into the bedroom. Fever was beginning to grip Squint. Dr. Dorris now had completed his daubing and bandaging and was gathering up his gauze and instruments in his small black bag.

"He'll sweat for a couple of days," the physician said unsympathetically. "He needs nursing, for he'll run a high fever."

"Where can I hire a nurse?" asked Brad from behind Newt Norton. "I want this man to have the best treatment possible."

"We got a shortage of nurses and hospitals in Shadrock," shrugged Dr. Dorris. "The best thing I can suggest is for you to make a deal with Miss Grace to let him stay here."

Brad turned to the girl. "I hate to ask it, but Squint here is pretty important to me."

Grace Coleman hesitated. She had her responsibilities to her uncle, and caring for a sick man was a full-time job. Now if it had been Brad Hunter wounded . . . Then she remembered her responsibility for Squint Elliott's plight. Perhaps her quick shot had been justified, but nevertheless she had wounded an innocent man. The strain of hearing the burglar, of shooting at him, of knowing the bank had been robbed of ten thousand dollars in cash and a deed, had taken its toll of her. She lifted a hand to her throbbing temple.

"I suppose so," she agreed. "But I hope you can find a nurse for him. I have enough work to do as it is between the bank and the store."

"Sure," Brad said quickly. "Any suggestions, marshal?"

"Maude Kimberlin is the smartest doctor in this valley," was the prompt answer.

"Including me," Dr. Dorris added. "If not Maude, bring her daughter in. The Kimberlins can use some money."

"And a man," murmured Newt, "who stands by while a burglar runs off with his ten thousand must have plenty of it."

"Enough to get by on awhile," Brad said curtly. Then

78

to Grace: "I'll stay with him until daylight. You go back to bed and grab some sleep. Then I'll ride out and hire Maude or her daughter to stay with him."

Squint opened his eyes. The foreman's face was flushed; the fever was setting in quicker than the doctor had predicted.

"And you don't dock my pay, you skinflint."

"Why should I?" shrugged Brad. "I've been paying you for three years for doing nothing. One week more won't make any difference."

Then the Tall T owner followed Newt outside again. "I suppose," he said, "you'll keep a lookout for the marked bills."

"What about the deed?" Newt asked.

"The deed ain't so important."

"You can get the bank to swear out a complaint if you got any evidence," Newt shrugged. "That is, if Luke Coleman is ever sober enough."

"We'll let it ride a couple of days," Brad decided. "I think you can pick up the trail without me."

"I dunno," the marshal said grimly. "I'm getting old. I don't see things as well as I used to."

The kid who called himself Montana helped Rooster bring up the remuda in the murky dawn of that morning and then announced to Pecos, who had just ridden in from an unexplained night mission and was acting foreman in Squint's absence, that he was leaving.

"Gotta catch on steady," he stated with dignity. "This just hanging around is no work for a man."

"Sure thing, kid," Pecos grinned. "Come around and feed your face again."

Montana rode over the ridges toward the Sloping S

ranch. He had heard of Ed Martin's outfit, which paid fifty and sixty a month instead of the usual forty. And he heard talk of Cherry Carr, Martin's riding boss, who was double-tough with men and double-sweet with women. That was what Montana wanted to be. He was young, but he knew how to handle his guns; and nobody buffaloed him on account of his age and size.

The rumors he had heard about Ed Martin's ways of running a spread didn't bother him at all. A man was a sap not to throw his branding iron on every calf he saw. That was the way to get ahead. And, if a man was tough enough, he could get by with it. Montana had been disappointed in Brad Hunter and Squint Elliott. He had figured that an outfit up from Texas must be as salty as a wild bronc'. But they were plumb gentle people. He had gotten by with talk in the Texan camp he wouldn't have dared pull in a Wyoming saloon.

He reached the headquarters of Ed Martin's Sloping S just before dawn. Ed was not there, nor Jinx Duval; but Cherry Carr was just getting his breakfast, and Hogshead Turpin, with an indulgent grin, ushered Montana in to the riding boss.

Montana gave Cherry a quick piercing study. Yeah, here was the type of man he wouldn't mind taking orders from. Young, and as tough as leather.

"I'm looking for a job," he announced.

Cherry grinned. "Yeah?" he drawled. "Doing what?"

"Get that grin off your face, you redheaded maverick," snapped Montana. "I can outrope you, outride you, and give you a run for your money any time you wanna grab your leather."

That was the way to get started with a new outfit—let 'em know right off that in spite of his age and size he didn't intend to stand for any foolishness. For a moment Cherry

Carr was speechless. Then he was angry with the quick hot anger of a man who is proud of his own toughness. With an older man, or a bigger boy, Cherry would have been unable to control himself. Now, after wrestling with his fury, he merely grinned again.

"There might be shooting," he said. "And if you don't wanna play rough, don't throw in your hat."

"I can ride and I can shoot," Montana said hotly. "If you got any doubts about either, speak your piece."

"Listen, button," growled Cherry. "We don't like fresh kids around here. Close your lip if you wanna get along with this outfit."

"Then I'm hired?"

"I don't know. I don't do the hiring. Ed should be back any minute. Go in and feed your face if you're hungry."

Montana accepted the invitation. He explained to the unimpressed cook that he was a tough riding hombre and just blew, and he would take this outfit to pieces if anybody got gay with him.

Then he returned to the bunkhouse porch. Cherry and the boys were waiting for Ed.

The black-bearded man came galloping up from the valleys with Jinx Duval. His face was stern, and Cherry, who knew his employer's moods, sensed that something had gone wrong, something serious.

"Who's this button?" demanded Martin, jabbing Montana's chest.

"They call me Montana," snapped the kid. "Do you want another rider, or don't you?"

Jinx Duval slouched forward and gave the boy a once-over. Recognition dawned on him.

"Say, weren't you down at the Texans' camp? working their remuda for 'em?"

"What if I was?" snapped back Montana. "I ate supper

and breakfast with 'em. They didn't have a job for me, so I rode on up here."

Martin studied the boy with bloodshot accusing eyes. In the mood he was in he was glad to find an object for his wrath.

"You look like a sniveling spy to me," he growled.

"I'm nobody's man," the kid said hotly. "I picked up a meal there and gave them a jump with their remuda. Any harm in that?"

"Could be," Ed snarled.

His lips parted in a savage grin. "I know how to treat spies," he threatened.

"I'm no spy," Montana claimed.

"Shut up," Ed roared, and knocked the kid off his feet with a hard swing.

Montana came up spitting blood and grabbed at his gun; but Cherry caught him from behind and disarmed him.

"So you'd gun me, damn you," growled Ed. He reached for his rope and tossed the loop over the kid's head, tightening it with a savage jerk. Then he leaped into his saddle, and before Cherry could protest the young rider was yanked off his feet and pulled headlong through the rocks and debris of the Sloping S clearing.

Cherry turned back to the bunkhouse. He didn't want to watch.

In a quarter-hour Ed returned, breathing heavily. "I pulled him down toward the Texan camp," he panted. "They'll find him today. Mebbe the next spy won't like his job."

"Kinda rough, weren't you?" Cherry murmured.

"I ain't ever claimed to be anything but rough," snapped Ed.

Chapter Seven

BRAD RODE HURRIEDLY toward their camp pitched at the mouth of Frenchman's Creek. Grace Coleman had pretended to nap for an hour or more, then had arisen and agreed to take charge of the patient until Brad could return with Maude or Katie Kimberlin. Squint was almost delirious from his high fever, and Brad cursed this unexpected turn of fate as he rode along. Nothing was worth losing Squint.

He sang out a greeting to a shadow which bolted toward him out of the darkness. Though there had been no inkling of trouble from the Sloping S crew, the Texans were keeping double night guard, and at the first sign of discord every man would be in the saddle, ready for riding or shooting.

"Hi, boss," greeted the rider. "Pecos just came in asking about you."

"Fine. How's it going?"

"Peaceful as all get-out. This Wyoming is a purty country—at night."

"Cows quiet?"

"Shucks, yes! Getting so fat they wobble."

Brad rode on to the fire, where Pecos Campbell was downing his third cup of coffee.

"That danged Limpy," growled Campbell, "wouldn't get up; and I had to brew my own poison. It stinks, Brad, but it's wet."

Brad produced his own tin cup and opened a can of condensed milk. One taste of the coffee, and he poured in more cream.

"Squint got hit," he said tersely. "Buckshot."

"You don't say! Gonna make it all right?"

"Reckon so. Left him at that Coleman's house. I gotta fan out here and dig up a nurse for him."

"The lucky son," growled Pecos. "Just buckshot—and you find him a nurse." The grizzled rider sighed. "Just a galoot born to luck. Here I gotta chase a danged waddy to hell and breakfast while he goes to bed in town just because of some buckshot."

"Got fever. You wouldn't change places with him."

"He won't die," avowed Pecos. "He'll live to hang."

The Tall T owner grinned. Squint never spoke a good word for a Tall T rider, and vice versa. Yet his crew's loyalty was as much Squint's doing as his own.

"Did you chase our friend who visited the bank clear back to his roost?"

"Yeah. And almost got in trouble. Had a compadre waiting for him just out of town."

Brad nodded. He had guessed that.

"They went right up to the Sloping S ranch," continued Pecos. "I just got back from tailing 'em."

Brad stirred his coffee with a tin spoon. It would take still more condensed cream to make it palatable. "Figgered as much. Reckon Mr. Martin is all put out right about now."

Pecos eyed his boss curiously. "Heard you and Squint talking," he apologized. It wasn't in his nature to pry into another man's affairs. Brad could tell him what to do and didn't have to explain why. "Ten thousand bucks of yours was in that wallet, wasn't it?"

Brad nodded. Pecos whistled and dipped his head. "Right smart money to ride on a hunch," he murmured. To a trail rider this was an incomprehensible sum.

"It's all marked," Brad grinned. "Oughta get most of it

84

back." He tasted the coffee again and frowned. "I don't think, Pecos," he drawled, "you had better ever break a leg. You can't make it as a camp cook, and all we could do with you is shoot you."

"And take aim careful-like," grunted Campbell. "I'd rather die an honest man's death than be a blankety-blank camp cook. Some day I'm gonna forget my good nature and throw that danged Limpy into a cactus bed."

Brad stood up with a sigh. He still had riding to do. "You're in charge while Squint is laid up," he said, with the crispness of authority in his voice. He ran this outfit, and nobody ever doubted it. "Same orders. Keep the cows in these flats. Keep the boys in camp unless I send for 'em. I'll bring 'em out some likker, and they can wet their whistle."

"Out here!" wailed Pecos. "Brad, that ain't no way to treat self-respecting cow hands. They wanna shine up to a purty girl and down their likker with their elbows leaning on a bar."

"We won't stay here forever," Brad promised. "That was the deal they came up here on. They gotta stick."

"I guess they'll stand it," grumbled Pecos.

"Are you keeping a lookout on the Sloping S ranch?"

"Night and day," Pecos nodded.

"Double it from now on," Brad ordered. "I wouldn't be surprised but what Ed Martin does some tall stirring around today."

He had unbuttoned his shirt collar against the warmth of the fire; now he pulled it tight. "I gotta mosey along," he explained. "Guess I'll be hard to catch for a couple of days. If you want me, send word to Miss Coleman. I'll be dropping on Squint pretty regularly."

"If you get your hide blasted," growled Pecos, "it's

nobody's fault but your own. We got the boys to clean up that outfit right quick. This tomfooling around ain't doing anybody any good."

"We'll see."

"When do you sleep?" demanded Pecos as the Texan started for his horse.

"I ain't sleepy," Brad grinned. "That one cup of coffee will keep me awake for a week."

He changed horses at the remuda, taking a big black mare that had durability and speed but never the sabby to be much of a cow pony. Then he cut across the creek, splashing through water hock-deep, and along the slopes leading back toward Sunrise Pass.

He had never ridden this country before; but it had been described to him in full detail, and he had no difficulty in locating the Kimberlin clearing and the small cabin which had never known paint or outside decoration. Daylight was just dropping over the pass when he pulled up and shouted "Hello."

After his third call he received a sleepy answer, and Maude Kimberlin came out of the hut in her cotton nightgown.

"Morning," he said pleasantly, removing his hat. "I got a hand laid up in town—at Miss Grace Coleman's. Got a load of buckshot. I'm after a nurse for him. Say for mebbe a couple of weeks."

He had dismounted and come close, courteously keeping his eyes on her face instead of the oversized body more exposed than protected by the limp shapeless nightgown.

Maude Kimberlin studied him closely. Beneath the nightgown her heart was pounding away at a trip-hammer pace. She didn't have to ask—this was the young Texan who had pushed his trail herd down Sunrise Pass.

86

"Reckon you can pay?" she asked calmly.

"Good," Brad nodded.

"I've done the nursing for this valley for twenty-five years," Maude said. "I think I've served my time. But I got a gal who can go. Will my daughter do?"

"I'd rather you came yourself."

"No," she answered after a moment's thought. There was a reason for her refusal that Brad Hunter couldn't guess. "Katie can tend to a sick man. If she can't now, she can learn."

"All right."

Without turning her head Maude bellowed, "Katie!"

"Yes, Maw?"

"Comere."

"I ain't dressed, Maw," came the wail from inside the cabin.

"Then git dressed," Maude Kimberlin snapped. "And don't take all day."

In a few moments Catherine was outside, shivering in the morning air as nothing covered her plumpness except a thin cotton dress.

"This gentleman wants to hire you to nurse a friend of his in town," Maude explained. "You'll stay with Miss Grace a few days. Pack what things you need."

"Yes, Maw," was the meek answer.

"Do you good," Maude snorted. "Get you away from that Cherry Carr. And the Lord knows we can use the money."

"Could you drive her in?" Brad asked. "I got another stop to make. And she'll want her things."

He reached into his pocket and pulled out two gold pieces. "That should take care of the bill for a little while," he said.

Maude Kimberlin gasped. "Forty dollars! Stranger, no nurse is worth that."

"I want my friend to have special care," Brad said gently, pushing the money upon her. "There will be more later."

Then he turned back to his horse. "We'll have breakfast in two shakes of a jack rabbit's tail," Maude invited, holding the coins tight in her coarse wrinkled hand. Already she was planning what to do with the money. She would send in one gold piece by Katie to pay on their overdue account at Luther Coleman's.

"Some other time," Brad grinned. "Right now I gotta travel. Get the girl into town as quickly as you can. Miss Grace says she has to stay with the bank and can't handle our patient in the daytime."

"Right away," nodded Maude. "Cal! Cal Kimberlin! Stir your stumps, Cal. Hitch up the wagon. We gotta get into town right away."

"What in tarnation!" complained a sleepy voice from inside the cabin.

Brad Hunter rode away with a grin on his lips. So this was Maude Kimberlin, the nester's wife who had served practically every family in Sunrise Valley as a midwife. He chuckled. Drifting Dan hadn't used near enough words in describing her. And yet he would have known her anywhere from Dan's description.

He cut back through the pines and located the road leading up the slopes to the flat timbered benchland where, long years ago, Bill Bradley had laid out the headquarters of the Sloping S ranch. The sun was bobbing over the rim top as he mounted a rise and saw the corrals and buildings sprawled out before him. He stopped for a moment, and for some reason took off his hat and stood bareheaded, as if he saw something here which no other human eye could make out; and his lips moved as if a voice was speaking to him which no other ear could catch.

Then, with a frown for the untidiness and the run-down condition, he rode slowly toward a low rambling frame building that was the Sloping S bunkhouse. Ed Martin had never married, and he had never rebuilt the house that had been burned twenty-five years ago, that now was a sodden black mass of ruins partially concealed by spreading blue stem.

Brad Hunter's roving glance saw these ruins, and his lips tightened. He snorted indignantly as he further observed the lack of care—the vines growing in confusion, thorny cactus sticking out, the warped corral fences. Tin cans were strewn all around, with other litter and refuse, until there was even a smell here; and he wondered how men, even Ed Martin's type of man, could have lived here this long without cleaning it up.

A voice sang out: "Who the hell are you?"

Brad turned to see a short bowlegged man walking out from the corrals with a Winchester slung over his arm.

The Texan rolled out of his saddle. "Out riding," he explained. "Thought it must be breakfast time."

There was nothing wrong with his calm assumption that he would be welcome. Since when, in a cattle country, wasn't any drifting man welcome for breakfast?

"Yeah? Who are you?"

"Name is Brad Hunter. I'm running the spread camped down at the creek."

"And yuh got the gall to come here for breakfast!" exploded the bowlegged man.

Then he lowered his rifle with a grin of appreciation. Men of his type always had a sense of humor. Nothing else kept them going. "Why not?" he asked. "Far as I'm concerned, stranger, you're plumb welcome. Course Ed might have something to say agin it."

"Where is Martin?"

"Hey, Ed, there's a waddy to see you," the bowlegged man yelled.

There was a snarling answer, and then Ed Martin stepped out of the bunkhouse. He was still in his undershirt, and his eyes were red and swollen as if he had not slept.

Then his eyes lost their crimson shade and became black evil glints as he recognized Hunter.

"What do you want?" he demanded. He took a half-step backward and felt to see if his gun was in its holster.

"Just riding by," Brad explained. He pulled the mixings out of his shirt pocket and rolled a smoke, his eyes meanwhile blandly studying his surroundings as if it were a natural thing for him to be here.

"Yeah? Why not keep riding?" snarled Martin.

"You seem to have me down wrong, Martin," the Texan grinned. "I'm just paying a sociable visit."

"You're no friend of mine, Hunter. You got cattle on my land. They won't stay there long. But mebbe you won't live to drive 'em back where you came from."

"I wanted to talk about that," murmured Brad. "The other day I asked Norton if you had a deed to this ranch. You ain't answered that question, Martin."

"The hell I haven't. My deed is on deposit at Luke Coleman's bank."

"Seems like," Hunter said slowly, "all the deeds in Wyoming are on deposit there. I left a paper there yesterday, Martin. The bank was burglared last night. My deed is gone."

"Yeah? Well, I dunno anything about it."

"Mebbe," Brad nodded. "I ain't claiming you broke in

the bank, Martin. I just wanted to ride by and tell you I'm offering a reward for the return of that deed. No questions asked."

"If I see anybody with a deed answering your description," growled Ed, "I'll send him around. Now suppose you ride on."

Cherry Carr sauntered out, brushing against his disturbed employer as Ed groped for the bunkhouse door. Martin was like that when mad, unable to see a foot in front of him.

"Riding far, ain't you?" drawled Cherry.

"Not so far," grinned Brad. "You look plumb rested, Red. Guess you stay home nights and get your sleep instead of gallivanting all over the country."

"Yeah," admitted Cherry, a twinkle in his eyes. "I stay home—where it's healthy. You might take some of that advice to yourself, Hunter."

"Might," nodded the Texan. "Remind me to buy you a drink sometime."

He swung back into his saddle and loped off. Cherry Carr stared after him a moment, then returned to the bunkhouse. A thin partition made Ed Martin a rough sort of office; in it the Sloping S owner was staring at a sheet of blank paper.

"What in hell do you want?" he scowled at Cherry.

"Your deal didn't work out," mused Cherry, sitting atop the wide board shelf which served Ed as a desk.

"So what?"

"I overheard part of Brad's talk. Everybody around here seems to be mouthing about a deed. A deed to what? The Sloping S?"

"I ain't saying. You dealt yourself out of this hand, Cherry. Stay out."

The red-haired man ignored Ed's bluntness. "Who did the job for you last night—Duval?"

"Yes."

"But he didn't get what you wanted?"

"No," admitted Ed. Then, blazing fire: "What the hell business is it of yours? You told me last night you were just a riding boss. Stay in your own pew, Cherry."

Cherry rolled a smoke and studied his employer's angry face with cool eyes.

"Don't go off the handle, Ed," he drawled. "I ain't robbing banks for nobody. But as long as I'm riding for the Sloping S I'll slap your brand on everything you say. You ain't doubting that, are you?"

"No," Ed conceded. "You're a good hand, Cherry."

"Then why not spill the beans?" the redhead demanded. "What has got you grabbing leather here all of a sudden? The talk is getting around the boys, Ed. They think you're buffaloed. That ain't good. You know what kind of boys they are. They don't ride for anybody but the top man. It ain't healthy to, the way they ride. Don't let 'em see you slipping. When they get the notion you're on your way out, they'll beat you over the hill. You'll look up all of a sudden, and there ain't anybody here but you."

"How about you?"

"You'll be by yourself, Martin," was the crisp answer.

"Yeah, I know," growled Ed. "Double-crossing rats, all of you. I figgered you were better than most, Cherry."

"If you make a play," shrugged the foreman, "I'll stand with you till hell freezes over. If you start running, I'll show you how to fan the breeze. What's the deal, Ed? Has this Texan got a deed to your ranch?"

"I don't know," confessed Ed Martin. He walked to the partition and looked around carefully. None of the other

Sloping S hands were in hearing distance. They had answered the cook's call to breakfast.

He decided to take Cherry into his confidence. In the first place, he could trust the redhead—at least not to make a play against him. In the second, he wanted to talk to somebody about what was worrying him.

"There ain't ever been a deed to the Sloping S that we could locate," he said tonelessly. "Luke Coleman and I worried about it. Specially Coleman. That was the main reason why he pulled out and went into town. He was scared. I split with him, giving him the fall cattle sales. He took that, resigned as sheriff, and started his bank and store."

"There is talk," murmured Cherry, "that Luke didn't think he got all that was coming to him."

"There is no proof of that," Martin said sharply. "Luke got all he was entitled to."

"I was just a button then," said the redhead. "Some of the details, I ain't learned. You and Luke and some of Jupiter Cross's boys ganged up on this Bill Bradley, who was pushing his herds every which way. You smoked him out, and him and his folks died in the fire. The waddy that gave you the most trouble was called Drifting Dan Thompson. You got him, too."

"The house burned quick," answered Ed. "Bill Bradley was killed, we know. We let his wife get out with two kids, and they went to Maude Kimberlin's. They died there a couple of days later. Scarlet fever. Dan Thompson was hit, and we figgered he died in the fire."

"But now," surmised Cherry, "this Texan comes up here talking about a Drifting Dan Thompson, and you ain't sure. You think mebbe Drifting Dan might have got away with Bill Bradley's deed to the Sloping S. And if this Texan has such a deed, and comes forward with his claim, you ain't got a prayer."

"I won't give it up," Ed flared. "The law can't run me out either."

"Did the Texan deposit his deed with Luke Coleman? That was what you wanted when you sent Jinx to rob the bank, wasn't it?"

"He got this," Ed said, handing over a sheet of paper. It was blank except for printing in pencil which read:

"Now we're even, you double-crosser."

Cherry chuckled. "It ain't funny," snapped his employer.

"Yep, it's funny," insisted Cherry. "The danged waddy was just fooling with you."

"Was he?" Ed asked thoughtfully. "I wish I could be sure. He made plenty of talk about his deed. He dropped strong hints, and Luke Coleman come running to me telling me about it. But mebbe Luke snitched the deed himself."

"Say!" exclaimed Cherry. "I hadn't thought of that."

"Luke claims I gypped him. Mebbe he took the deed and left this note. Mebbe he's got the paper to the Sloping S and is sitting down there in his bank grinning like a fox about it."

"I'd still say," shrugged the redhead, "that this Texas hombre is the nigger in the woodpile. I don't believe Coleman has the guts to pull off anything like this."

"Yeah, I see that," nodded Martin. "This Texan has the men to jump us out. If the law was on his side, with his deed, would he be holding back? For some reason he ain't in a hurry. I'd give a pretty penny to be sure, Cherry."

Cherry thought a minute. "Mebbe he's just baiting you. His spread is strong, Ed. If you expect us to shoot it out with 'em any time you oughta bring in some boys."

"How can I?" sighed Ed. "This outfit ain't what it used to be. I'm in debt up to my neck now."

"I been telling you," Cherry pointed out, "that you don't sabby cattle. You overgrazed the range two years straight, Ed, and now you're paying the price. You oughta sell off some of your stockers and all of your culls and wait for the pasture to grow back. You need cross fences and some dams in the flats."

"We ain't got time for that—now," Ed said surlily. Cherry was always giving him advice about running the ranch. What galled him was that what his red-haired foreman predicted usually came true. "Unless I can lay my hands on that deed, or shoot up Hunter's gang, we ain't got a ranch."

"And you figger Coleman got the deed?"

"Yeah. Just like the dirty little rat. Probably holed up there in his damn bank drinking likker and laughing at me."

"How are you gonna get it away from Luke?"

"I been thinking," Ed mused. "Luke sets a heap by his niece, that blonde gal. Doubt if we could get to Luke himself without Newt Norton popping in. Newt has his ear to the wind, and he ain't about to be neutral. He was a friend of Bill Bradley and Drifting Dan Thompson, and he's been waiting his chance these long years. But I figger that, if we snatch Luke's niece, we could make him come across. We could stake her out in one of our line cabins on the rim until Luke comes across."

"And have the law on our necks? Kidnaping ain't funny, Ed."

"The law won't bother us," Ed growled. "Sam Dugan does what I tell him."

"But Newt Norton ain't Sam Dugan."

"It'll be out of Newt's jurisdiction," shrugged Martin. "He's just a marshal."

"You think of the damnedest things," sighed Cherry.

"Robbing a bank one night, stealing a gal the next day. Don't you ever do things the easy way, Ed?"

"Like what?"

"Run them Texans out," snapped Cherry. "Didn't you lift that ten thousand bucks the Texan deposited?"

"Yeah," Martin agreed reluctantly. "It was in the wallet. But Jinx didn't know he was stealing dough."

"Well, I guess that would have worried Jinx," said Cherry with heavy sarcasm. "He'd steal the ring off his dead grandmother's finger. But you got the dough. Ten thousand bucks?"

"Yeah."

"You can hire boys with that," grinned the redhead. "You're guilty of conspiring to rob a bank so you might as well spend the money and bluff it out. Send over to Laramie and pick up a dozen good hands. The Tipton gang is hanging out near there and they'd shoot up a bunch of Texans for little or nothing. Then you can let the boys go."

"I thought of that," Ed admitted. "I been thinking plenty. How about you taking the dough over to Laramie and hiring us some killers? You know the owl hooters better than I do."

"Jinx knows 'em better than me," Carr shrugged. "He practically sleeps with 'em."

"But I don't want to trust Jinx too far."

"Or me," grinned Cherry. "I ain't to be trusted with money. Now women—I'm different there. I know how to handle women. You want this Coleman gal picked up and carried to a line cabin and held there until her uncle comes across. That's the job for old Cherry, Ed. I can keep her entertained."

"If you hurt that gal, Cherry," Ed Martin said slowly,

"there would be hell to pay. I don't want to crowd this country too far. Jupiter Cross will stay out of my way 'cause he was in this at the start—he sent some of his riders over to help us burn out Bradley. Sledge Mahoney won't give a damn as long as I stay on this side of the river. But this country wouldn't stand for us mistreating a gal like Grace Coleman."

"I won't hurt her," Carr protested. "I might honey her up a little, that's all. She might like me after she gets to know me better. Most women do."

Ed sighed. "I sure hate to send Duval riding off with that dough."

"He won't pull out on you," Cherry said in disgust. "I'll talk to him if you want. He's scared to death I'm gonna jump him out anyhow."

"Do that," Ed agreed. "I gotta depend on you, Cherry. You're the only one in this outfit who's worth a damn."

"Sure, sure," the redhead grinned. "I'll grab the gal and carry her to that cabin up by dripping springs. Nice and quiet up there. We can have peace and privacy."

Chapter Eight

GRACE COLEMAN hailed Katie's arrival with genuine relief. Customers had been in and out of the store all morning —more to gab and sate their curiosity than to trade, it was true, but still taking her time and attention—and, of course, her uncle wasn't around to relieve her of the load. For an hour or more she had her fears about a run on the bank; no fewer than three people came in to draw out their accounts. But Newt Norton learned of this and stood outside the bank and assured all and sundry that only ten thousand dollars had been stolen, and this had been deposited in one package by the owner of the Texas trail herd. The three people who had drawn out their money brought it back, and Grace sighed in relief.

No cattle-country bank could have weathered such a campaign. Sledge Mahoney and Jupiter Cross owed Luther Coleman's establishment sizable sums, enough to throw the bank into bankruptcy if customers made a determined run.

Katie took charge of the patient just before noon. Grace received her with misgivings; she did not think that the plump-faced nester's daughter had the intelligence and industry to care for a patient. But she learned in short order that Catherine Kimberlin was a different girl away from her mother's domination. Though she reddened from this strange contact with a member of the opposite sex, she rolled Squint Elliott over and changed the bedclothes, then put the small house in order and within an hour's time after her arrival had dinner cooking on the stove.

On another day Grace might have resented the calm efficient way in which Catherine took over. Now she hailed Maude's daughter with a great relief. The strain of the night before and the short-lived but menacing run on the bank had taken its toll.

Dr. Dorris came by and redressed the patient's wounds. Squint's fever dropped, and by noon he was eating soup and sitting up with a grin for the physician's coarse gibes.

Then Grace saw Brad Hunter dismounting from his horse at the side gate and walked around the store to meet him.

"Your friend seems to be doing well enough," she said.

"I appreciate your trouble," he assured her. "You certainly have been kind to two drifting Texans."

"I'm only sorry that I shot him. It's been worrying me ever since."

"That couldn't be helped. We shouldn't have been hanging around the bank."

"I still haven't figured out why you didn't stop them," she said pointedly. Newt Norton, she knew, was wondering the same thing.

"We're just passing through," he shrugged. "Don't want to get mixed up in Wyoming people's squabbles."

Newt himself walked up.

"Got the burglar yet?" Brad asked.

"Strange," the marshal said slowly. "Can't pick up his trail anywhere. I may have to listen to your suggestions yet, Hunter."

"We stand for law and order," smiled the lean man. "I'd like to run in and see Squint if it isn't too much trouble, Miss Coleman. I know how you feel about people tracking up your house. Just shoo me out if I ain't welcome."

"You're always welcome," she assured him.

A red spot leaped in each cheek as she realized how over-eager she had sounded.

Brad spoke pleasantly to Catherine Kimberlin, and likewise noticed a change in the nester's girl. She had seemed a nonentity to him that morning in front of Cal Kimberlin's cabin. But she had color and a pleasing personality—shy, yes, but since when has a man objected to that? She came quietly in to take Squint's soup and to bring the patient a cup of coffee.

"Podner, how about changing places with me?" Brad asked before her.

"Don't crowd me, friend," Squint declined. "I ain't had so much fun since roundup at the XIT ranch. I don't know where you picked up this nurse of mine, but you can have my best saddle and wear my new hat to a dance at Danny's sometime."

There was a pleased gleam in Catherine's eyes which showed she didn't mind the palaver, despite the crimson spots in both cheeks. She returned to the kitchen and presently asked Grace: "Mr. Hunter is still in there. Shouldn't we ask him to stay for dinner?"

"By all means."

Brad hesitated, then accepted. It was past noon already and he didn't want to ride back to the camp until late afternoon. Then there would be no chance of a meal until supper. Limpy prepared extra meals for no man, not even Brad Hunter. Even a ranch owner had to tread carefully where the camp cook was concerned. Limpy, like all of his kind, feared no man and resented the hand of authority.

Katie had cooked fried apple pies and, to a man used to trail fare, this was luxury indeed.

"You ain't done nothing to deserve treatment like this," he growled at Squint as he left.

Grace Coleman walked with Brad to the gate. For a man who had lost ten thousand dollars in cash and an important deed, he did not seem very worried.

"I hope," she murmured, "that Newt can get your money back. Sam Dugan, the sheriff, is still out of town. But Sam won't do anything when he does get back. Newt is our only hope."

"Don't worry too much about it," he grinned.

"Is money that plentiful in Texas? that losing ten thousand dollars doesn't upset you?"

"A funny thing about that money," he murmured. "It never was exactly mine anyhow. I brought it along to do a job for me. And I think it will."

She studied his face a moment, then decided against asking for a further explanation. All along, there had been something of a riddle about the way this young Texan came over the pass with his trail herd. Tongues would wag until he had gone. But not hers. A western man didn't like women who couldn't conceal their curiosity. And it was very, very important that Brad Hunter should like Grace Coleman.

"Whatever it is you came to Shadrock for, Brad, I hope you find it," she murmured.

It was the first time she had called him "Brad." The name slipped off her lips before she thought. He didn't seem to notice it. He grinned his appreciation of the dinner he had eaten and went riding off, his mind intent on another errand. She returned to the store and half-heartedly began to mark down slow-moving items for a special sale. A woman must get used to that. There are times when a man has no place in his life for a woman, any woman. It is not a snub or a rebuke, and the woman who makes it that must pay the price of stubborn unyielding insistence. Particularly so in this country where a man must by necessity ride a long way from home, and must, even while sitting at his own fireside, hold fresh the memory of hills and trails a woman is never privileged to know.

A woman cannot stand such treatment except from one man; with no other does she understand it. Newt Norton came into the store and purchased a handful of cigars and studied Grace with his unblinking glance.

"The Texan," murmured the marshal, "throws a pretty mean loop."

She started to deny his insinuation with indignation, then admitted the charge with a blush and a nod. At a time like this she felt alone. There was only Luther Coleman in the whole world, and he was sleeping off his nightly drunk in Fatty's private room.

Into the store bustled Cora Snodgrass, the wife of the saddle maker. There was talk about the bank robbery while Cora examined the dress goods just received on the stage. She bought a small piece of calico, but it was obvious that she had come to pass on what information she had stored up, and to press Grace Coleman for more.

"I wouldn't be surprised," sniffed Cora, "if those Texans didn't rob the bank themselves and are just pulling the wool over Newt Norton's eyes. More outlaws come from Texas than from anywhere else. Never saw a man from Texas who wasn't a wild one."

Grace smiled indulgently. Cora Snodgrass could babble on and on without upsetting her.

"This Brad Hunter would be more put out than he is if he had lost ten thousand dollars," continued the saddlemaker's wife. "Why, right this minute he is down at

Ramona's. A man who's been robbed of that much money would be out looking for it instead of down at that hussy's."

Grace could not ignore this. Brad at Ramona's! She tried to conceal from Mrs. Snodgrass how this had hit home. Cora studied her narrowly, but could only guess that Luther Coleman's niece was upset by this declaration.

"We sure hope, honey," said Cora solicitously, "that you don't make the mistake of falling for either of these Texas drifters. They're out for no good."

"I believe," Grace said icily, "that I can take care of myself, Cora."

"We're worried about you, all of us," went on Mrs. Snodgrass, ignoring this very strong reproof. "You with no father nor mother and only that drunken uncle of yours."

"Is that all, Cora?"

"Why, yes. Oh, I forgot—a spool of white thread. No. 9."

Mrs. Snodgrass bustled off, and Grace continued her marking with even less enthusiasm for the job. So Brad Hunter was at Ramona's. Possibly there was no harm in that. Cowboys into town on pay day usually ended up there. The half-breed girl who was all that was left of Ramona's once elegant retinue was considered attractive. Grace had never seen her. Ramona stayed in Shadrock after others of her type had been driven out because she kept her house concealed from view of the townsmen and her girls strictly off Shadrock's too-narrow streets.

Once Ramona's place had been well kept, and even fashionable. Then, when the silver mines were running full blast, she had kept as many as a dozen girls, some of them straight out of San Francisco, and she had carried her gold dust to the bank in a heavy canvas bag. No one had ever known why Ramona stayed on after the boom collapsed. Shadrock, hemmed in on three sides by the towering mountains and the badlands, with rugged Sunrise Pass as its only outlet, had no need of a place such as hers, and certainly did not support it in the manner to which Ramona and her girls had been accustomed. But there she stayed through slow tedious years, and now she must be past forty-five and close to fifty, although old-timers still remembered how young she had looked when she came to Shadrock, and how some of the town's best people had been taken in by her baby stare.

The years had dealt with her lightly, in direct contrast to the treatment time usually hands out to her kind. The half-breed girl, sulking on the front porch and considering moving to Fort Laramie where the red lights burned bright and for long hours after the soldiers were paid, saw Brad first, and ran out to meet him.

Once there had been a Mexican boy to take a visitor's horse; but Ramona's customers could not expect such service these days. There was a brass-studded hitching post, given to the madam by a dust-rich miner just back from a spree in Denver. Brad Hunter looped his horse's reins over the brass knob and shook his head at the half-breed's protestations that she was clean, and that he was bound to want a woman.

"I'd like to talk to Ramona," he said.

"Just talk!" pouted the half-breed. She was a pretty little wild thing, more Indian in coloring and features than white. "All you men—just talk. How you expect girls to make a living?"

"I'll let my boys come in some night," smiled Brad. "They'll be glad to know there's a pretty girl like you around."

This had been a two-storied house once, with all rooms full of giggling womanhood and blazing lamps. Now only the downstairs was used, and Ramona must share the household duties with her companion. The rugs were shabby, and the furniture chipped, and the gilt on the fixtures and staircase railing tarnished to a mangy brown. Luther Coleman had offered Ramona a handsome price for this residence before his wife had died and his business had dropped; but she had refused. It had been Shadrock's finest house once and could be again.

Ramona had a dust rag in her hand and a bandanna wrapped around her hair. A soiled negligee hung loosely, and carelessly, from her shoulders, and Brad saw that she was still a fine figure of a woman, still enough to stir a man's blood in spite of the long years. With her hair curled, with powder and make-up, in a long clinging gown, she would still resemble, in a soft kind light, the Ramona Custer that old-timers remembered, and that one Drifting Dan Thompson had talked about in his last years.

"Ramona Custer?" asked Brad with a respect which the half-breed girl did not receive from visitors, but which Ramona usually did. Somehow she still retained the qualities that compelled men to address her politely. "My name is Brad Hunter. I'm from Texas. I'm a friend of Drifting Dan Thompson."

Ramona's eyelids flickered. All her life, she had kept her honest emotions locked up, answered men's talk with an automatic smile that meant nothing, and purposely meant nothing. But now her hands trembled and her body shook; and, for a second, her eyes closed tightly. It wasn't fair to remind a woman so suddenly, and so violently, of her memories.

"Yes?" she murmured.

"Dan died about a year ago," Brad said awkwardly. He had dreaded this assignment—of carrying to this woman called Ramona the last message of a gunman who had loved her. "He never forgot you. He made me promise to come to see you if I ever got up to Wyoming."

Ramona was studying his face with her deep dark eyes. There was a hint of Indian blood in her, but only enough to make her coloring dark and rich. There wasn't even the suggestion of a gray hair in her head. Brad, knowing how old she must be, had come expecting to see her beauty had been utterly squandered, leaving nothing but a hollow shell of artificiality.

She turned to the half-breed girl. "Bring Mr. Hunter a drink," she said with quiet dignity. "We will have it in my sitting room."

She led the way down the corridor into a small room opening off the back porch. Here, Brad knew, she had entertained her special friends, men like Drifting Dan who could not enter through the front door because their presence might be reported to the law; but the young Texan did not know that here also came Newt Norton by habit as soon as dusk had fallen to visit for an hour or more with the one true friend he had in Shadrock—or that here, on occasional evenings, came Ed Martin with money to spend and liquor to gulp.

The half-breed brought his drink and was sent out with a nod. "Sit there," said Ramona, pointing to a rocking chair, and took a plush-covered stool at his feet.

Brad's eyes moistened. Dan Thompson had told him about the way she sat at a man's feet, looking up with deep grave dark eyes, always listening. ("There never was a woman in all the West," Drifting Dan had vowed, "who could listen as sweet.")

106

He sipped his drink. It was hard to say what he had to say.

"Dan told me," he murmured, "to let you know that he was sorry to his death that you didn't go with him to Texas."

Ramona nodded. "You are the boy he carried with him?" she guessed.

"Yes."

"And you have driven a herd back to Sunrise Valley? Why? To pick up your father's fight?"

"Yes."

"I was always afraid Dan would come back himself," she said slowly. "He promised not to. But so few men can keep their promises. Dan is the only one I ever knew who could."

"He kept it," Brad nodded. "He made the same promise to Mrs. Bradley—my mother. He did well in Texas. He had ten thousand dollars to start with, and he was a born cattleman. The Tall T was staked out in my name, but it was Dan who built it up. Now I own a ranch that a man can't ride across in one day. I couldn't guess within a thousand how many cows we'll drive north next spring. I guess I'm rich, though a boy who was raised by Dan Thompson naturally doesn't worry about that very much."

"No," murmured Ramona.

He studied her face again. "Dan always grieved about you being up here—in this house. He said you wouldn't marry him because of danged-fool notions that women couldn't turn back on trails, that all that was left for them was the trail ahead. The money I have is due to Dan Thompson. I'd like to take you out of here. I even wish you'd come back to Texas with me."

Ramona Custer smiled. It was a gentle beautiful smile,

and the memory of it would haunt Brad Hunter for a long time. "You *are* like Dan," she murmured. "I can look at you and imagine you are Dan Thompson's son instead of Bill Bradley's."

Brad realized that she had been studying his face so intently that she hadn't heard a word of his proposal. He repeated it.

Ramona laughed softly. "Men, men! Always you think of ways to get me out of here. None of you ever realize that I'm here of my own choice. Look at me, Brad Hunter. Am I a weak wailing creature that you should take pity upon me and offer me the shelter of your corral?"

"No," Brad grinned. This woman had a personality, no doubt about it.

"For years I have entertained men, my friends," she said, waving her hand at the faded luxury of her small sitting room, "here in my own room. Many of them have expressed the same worries as you. What of poor Ramona when she grows old? What man can she cling to? Ramona has never clung to men. And, while Ramona is indeed getting old, the men she knew are older, and need my help today even more than I need theirs. And some of them are dead."

She was silent a moment. "How did Dan die?"

"Of pneumonia," Brad said promptly. "And he was old, you know. He must have been over forty when you knew him."

"Yes. And nearly blind. Everyone thought Newt Norton was so wonderful for shooting him down in front of the bank. Dan got the first shot, and missed. He was always glad. So was I. Newt became his closest friend. And mine."

She reached for a bell rope and pulled it. "You need another drink," she observed. "So do I. Dan Thompson!

Drifting Dan, the man with a price on his head, but with a soul money couldn't touch! I loved him, young Brad Hunter. I fell in love with him the first time he walked into my place. This very house."

"You should have gone to Texas with him."

"No," Ramona shrugged. "This is my life. But I've talked like an old woman. What of you, Brad Hunter? The bank was robbed last night, and your money and deed taken. What now?"

So she had heard of that. Brad's lips curved in a grin. "That was just a feint," he said calmly. "You see, Miss Ramona, my actions are kinda cramped up here. A promise I made to Dan."

Ramona Custer nodded. "Is that why you're not wearing a gun?"

Brad Hunter grinned. Dan Thompson had warned him that this woman saw through everything.

"Yes. I'm trying to pull a scheme."

"Tell me about it," she said, laying her hand on his knee. He hesitated.

"Don't be silly," smiled Ramona. "You're the closest thing to a son Drifting Dan Thompson and I ever had. I know the people in this valley. Tell me what your game is. And don't think for a moment Ramona Custer won't do all she can to help you."

Brad yielded. She listened with a glow in her dark eyes. "I think it will work," she said when he had finished.

Until now she had not touched her drink. She tossed it off with a quick gesture. "Ed Martin, Luke Coleman, Newt Norton! Newt is here almost every night. But Newt is clever. Ed Martin comes, too. I hate him, of course. I wish he would never come again."

"Then why let him?" Brad demanded.

Ramona sighed. "That is my way of life—letting all men come as long as they pay and don't disturb other customers. Ed Martin is a stupid man. He is a vain man. He has thought for a long time that I am in love with him. He has even offered, as you, to take me out of this house."

"Mine was a different kind of offer," Brad said hastily.

"Of course," Ramona laughed. She stood up and held out her hand. "Come again, Brad Hunter. And, as far as your intrigue is concerned, leave that to Ramona. Tell the spirit of Drifting Dan Thompson that you will settle for your father's murder without firing a gunshot."

"I shall," he murmured.

She turned and walked away from him. In a moment the half-breed girl came to show him out. Brad had been told about that, too—that Ramona ran her place with the regality of a great lady. The half-breed pushed against him.

"Come back sometime, mister," she urged. "My name's Jeanne. I'm good for what ails you."

"I'll think it over," Brad smiled. He pressed a coin into her hand.

She studied it a moment, then handed it back. "You got me wrong, friend," she snapped. "Keep your money, until I've earned it."

Brad sighed. Mebbe some day he would learn something about women.

It was hot in the flats, and Newt Norton stopped to wipe the perspiration from his face and let his horse water in the shallow creek. Then he rode on toward the rimside and the valley where Calvin Kimberlin and his brood tried to hide from Ed Martin's attention.

Maude was baking. He sniffed the hot rolls and accepted one. Nobody in this valley could make better bread than

Maude. She put her last batch of dough into the outdoor oven and then gave him a resentful look.

"If you're around to ask more questions about that fire," she snapped, "forget 'em. I've done all the talking I'm going to."

"Just visiting," Newt denied. "Where's Cal?"

"Cutting fence posts up on the ridge. Go up and talk to him. He's always glad for somebody to come by to gab with. Gives him an excuse to stop chopping. Not that he doesn't have a hundred already."

Newt rode on with a faint smile. But he was not going to go into the pines and palaver with Cal Kimberlin. Behind the cabin, in a small valley through which trickled one of the small springs which formed Frenchman's Creek, he found what he was searching for.

Here was the Kimberlin graveyard. Newt clucked in approval as he saw that it had been fenced off with cedar posts against drifting cattle, and that the brush had been cut away. Pine slabs turned to dingy gray by the rains and winds of twenty-five years marked the three graves. Caskets had been provided by sympathetic Shadrock people, but not tombstones. The inscriptions had been carved into the pine slabs by Cal's own jackknife.

Newt bent over and laboriously figured out Cal's crude lettering.

"Juanita Bradley."

So this was the grave of Bill Bradley's wife, who had fled in terror with two sick children to the shelter of Maude Kimberlin's small cabin, and had died there.

"Elizabeth Kimberlin."

This was the child that had died at the same time, only a few months old. Newt remembered drinking with Doc Dorris on the night she was born. There had been some trouble in delivery, and the young physician was whooping it up in gleeful relief. Both Maude and the baby had come through fine. Even though he would never get a nickel, Dr. Dorris celebrated the triumph over death.

There was no etching on the third slab. Newt picked it up to make sure. He replaced it carefully. Maude had also lost a boy in that scarlet fever scourge just after the fire. But it was strange that Calvin Kimberlin had not carved a headstone for his own son.

Chapter Nine

DUVAL LISTENED to his boss with appraising eyes. So Ed Martin wanted to hire more riders for the Sloping S. That meant he expected trouble with the Texans, and pronto.

Already they had talked in the bunkhouse, when Ed and Cherry were not there. Their kind of outfit had to have heavy odds in their favor. They were paid to shoot straight and to kill, but not to fight man to man. They were not afraid—no more than the average rider; but they were acutely aware of the percentage, and tried to play it as cannily as a gambling-house dealer. If it was a fifty-fifty show, it did not pay them to be mixed up in it. Better to ride on to another spread and another range war where the scales would be tilted in their favor.

This was not disloyalty. They were indifferent to Ed Martin as a man and the Sloping S as an outfit. In a game like theirs personalities couldn't be figured. A man just had one life to sell; he had to sell it as many times as he could, and even then he didn't get paid too well for it. The pay was so little, considering that risk, that many such riders wavered back and forth across the thin wavering line that separated the owl-hoot trail from the law-abiding road, without the recklessness to stay on one side or the patience to endure the other.

"If you double-cross me by skipping out with this dough," growled Ed, "I'll follow you to hell and back. I'll send Cherry after you."

"Aw, button your lip," drawled Duval. "Nobody is gonna run off with your dough."

He was offended by Ed's suspicion. He had his code, and stealing from his employer was decidedly against it. Ed Martin never gave his men enough rope. He knew where they came from, and he was afraid to trust them. He would not concede them a type of honesty and faithfulness which most of them had.

Duval tied the money in his slicker and rode toward the pass. He rather relished the job ahead of him, though Ed's suspicions made him sullenly resentful. He wouldn't fan the breeze—Ed could depend on that, and take it or leave it.

High up on the pass Dollar Bill Dunlop and Julian Vega, two of Brad's most trusted riders, were on the alert for suspicious comings and goings around the Sloping S headquarters. They saw Duval ride toward the pass, turning away from the fork which led into Shadrock, and knew that this was something about which they had better notify their employer posthaste. Dollar Bill mounted his pony and galloped for the Texans' camp while Julian took up his post just around one of the pass's narrowest bends.

Brad was in town, but Pecos Pete Campbell had full instructions as to what should be done.

"Grab the waddy and bring him in," he snapped. "Flint, Comstock, Rosey—give Dollar a jump."

"It would be just like that danged Julian," grumbled Dollar Bill, "to have the son eating out of his hand when we get there."

Flint, Comstock, and Rosey were as eager for action. This sitting around a camp got on a man's nerves. Brad could keep them rustling their bottoms, but he couldn't make them like it.

They saw Duval high above them, climbing up the steep

winding pass, and knew they would never reach him before he stumbled into Julian Vega.

"Hope the danged Spick don't get hurt," growled Dollar Bill. "He ain't much of a hand, but we'd miss that git-tar of his."

And his braiding. Julian was a favorite with the Tall T boys.

"Hell, don't worry none about Julian," scoffed Rosey. "That guy can shoot the whiskers off a fly. He was a tough hombre in Piedras Negras."

Now Julian could hear the clatter of Duval's coming and was grinning. He pulled his horse against the rock ledge until he was almost hidden from any man approaching the peak of the pass, and waited.

Jinx Duval loped leisurely on, thinking about the spree he would throw in Fort Laramie. He wouldn't steal a dime of Ed Martin's money, but a man had the right to hold out a little for expenses. He had to buy drinks for some of the boys, didn't he? And mebbe play a little poker with 'em to win their confidence!

He reined up as he saw Julian's shadow. The Mexican waited motionlessly. Duval hesitated a moment, then rode on slowly. His narrow eyes studied Julian in hostile speculation. He didn't rate a Mexican too high. He had lived most of his life in the upper West and didn't know that in the border country a Mex gunman was held in respect.

"Where to, frien'?" Julian asked politely, flashing his white teeth as he grinned.

"Reckon that's a personal matter," Duval drawled. He slouched forward in his saddle and dropped his hand slightly in preparation for a slick draw. If this Spick gave him any trouble, he would drop him and cut off his ears. A Mexican's ear would be good for a drink in Fort Laramie.

"No," smiled Julian. "This road, she is closed."

"Yeah."

"*Sí*."

"Listen, you damned Spick!" raged Duval. "I'll—" his threat ended in a weak gasp. He had yanked at his gun as he spoke, but he found himself looking into the barrel of Julian's revolver before his was even clear of his holster. "Gawdamighty!" he murmured. If this was the kind of men who rode with Brad Hunter, he wanted no part of the Texans.

"As you gringos say, hands up!" smiled Julian.

Jinx Duval obeyed unhesitantly. It didn't occur to him to take a chance. This Mexican had the drop on him, and he wasn't arguing about it.

Dollar Bill, Comstock, and Rosey came galloping up, growling in disappointment.

"Might have known it," Dollar grumbled. "A greaser always gets the breaks."

Julian's smile broadened. These men always talked to him like that. But they were his friends, and he was never offended.

"I git him queeck," the Mexican boasted. "He try to pull gun on me—Julian Vega."

"That was your mistake, friend," Dollar Bill told Duval.

"Seems like." The Sloping S rider was cool about the whole situation. "Now what's the play, gents? I'm riding toward Fort Laramie on personal business. I ain't bothering you none, and I'll thank you to treat me the same."

"Your mistake," grinned Dollar Bill. "You're riding back to camp with us, and you are gonna stay there and act like a gentleman until the boss talks to you."

"Then what?"

"That's up to the boss."

Jinx Duval sighed. He didn't like to give up any more than the next man. Sooner or later they would get around to looking at his saddlebags, and the ten thousand dollars therein would be a dead give-away. Furthermore, the money was still in Brad's wallet.

"Don't get any notions," Dollar Bill said harshly as he noticed Duval's hesitation. "We don't wear these guns just to work the fat off our horses. One funny move out of you, and you ain't listed among the present population any longer."

They meant just that, Jinx decided. He shrugged his shoulders and submitted docilely. "O.K., gents. Lead on."

Back at the camp Pecos had sent a rider into town for the Tall T owner, and he reached the creek mouth just before Duval and his captors.

"Hate to interrupt your trip, Duval," he grinned, "but you were figgering on making it at my expense. Where's the dough—in your saddlebags?"

"You know so much about it, find it yourself," Jinx snarled. He was a little taken back by Brad Hunter's immediate sureness that he had been trying to carry the stolen money out of the valley.

Brad fished the wallet out of the slicker with a chuckle. "Duval, you were a rich man for a couple of hours, weren't you?"

"You got your dough," Duval snarled. "Now lemme out of here."

"You're staying here a spell," Brad said coldly. "When you do leave, you're riding into Shadrock—to face trial for burglary."

"Hey, you can't pin anything like that on me. What the hell, you're not a law man anyhow."

"It's my duty as a public-spirited citizen," Brad grinned,

"to turn you over to Newt Norton in the near future. Not for a couple of days. We want Ed Martin sweating for that long."

"Lemme get word to Ed," begged Duval.

"Not a chance," Hunter snapped. "Now pipe down before I have the boys slap a gag on you."

Jinx Duval subsided. He knew when the cards had been dealt against him.

Each dusk seemed to touch Shadrock with a fleeting gentleness, rolling quickly away from the heavier, more clinging banks of darkness. Newt Norton, on the courthouse steps, with a cigar between his teeth and almost a smile on his leathery face, watched the night roll in. Much of the jumbled puzzle that had shaken this Wyoming town out of its languor was working itself out. Any moment now Brad Hunter might show the color of his hole card. A charge could be sworn out against Ed Martin for conspiring to rob the bank just any moment. But the Texan was not disposed to hurry and Newt felt like matching his patience.

He saw Hunter ride up to the saloon, and walked in that direction. The Texan seemed to be racing from camp to town and back again.

Sloping S men also rode in, but without Ed Martin. Cherry Carr was in the lead, and he swaggered into Fatty's with a whoop of expectation. Newt quickened his pace. Brad Hunter did not seem to know the humor of this country. Sloping S men were apparently starting on a spree, and liquor always made men dangerous. There were fighting men in this Sloping S crew. Cherry Carr, for one.

The marshal sighed in relief as Brad left the saloon and

walked to the Coleman side gate. He nodded in approval and took his stance between Coleman's and the saloon. There could be trouble this night. Damn Hunter anyhow for not wearing a gun.

Brad found Squint Elliott sleeping. Toward sundown he came up with a fever, which Dr. Dorris had said was perfectly natural, and had a restless sleep. Catherine Kimberlin was watching over him closely, and Grace Coleman was washing dishes in the kitchen.

"Has the lady killer got you going yet?" Brad asked Katie.

Her blush told him that Squint was working on that angle. "Did he really have seven wives in Texas, Mr. Hunter?" the girl asked.

"Never got near enough a woman to touch her," Brad denied. "Don't believe a word Squint says. Not even if he says 'Good morning.'"

"Oh, I don't mind," she said. "I think he's a nice man."

"All wool and a yard wide," Brad said promptly. He studied her face again. "You oughta latch on to a man like him while you got the chance," he grinned. "Don't let him up till he promises to marry you."

"Oh, Mr. Hunter!"

He started out humming. Grace Coleman called after him and walked with him to the gate.

"We seem to have a match working in there," he smiled.

"I wouldn't doubt it," she agreed. "Your foreman can talk the arm off a wooden hobbyhorse."

"She would be getting a good man," Brad mused.

A random shiver of moonlight played across their faces, leaping from one to the other almost with their exchange of speech. Again he was stirred by the cool beauty of her, the calm sweetness that a man wants in a woman who will be there forever. And again he reminded himself that this was Luther Coleman's niece. She ran Luther's bank and his house, and there must come a time when she would hate Brad Hunter and what he stood for. It would be unfair to presume upon her until then.

"It's a beautiful night," she murmured.

"Yes, it is."

Grace turned to him with sudden decision. "It would be a wonderful night for a ride down by the river. There are rapids just above the pass that would be splendid by moonlight."

"I'm sure they are," Brad said stiffly. "Some night we must go for a ride."

But they wouldn't. The time would come when she would hate him, and fling that feeling into his face.

"Yes," Grace murmured, biting her lip, "some other time."

He was silent a moment, and then was slow and clumsy with his speech, as he was with his thoughts. "Squint seems to be getting along fine," he said.

"Yes. The doctor says he can rejoin his crew in two or three days. You'll like that, won't you?"

"Sure. We miss the galoot." He lifted his hat. "So long, Miss Grace. I'll drop in tomorrow."

"So long," she answered back, her voice dull and flat.

She sat on the steps a long time after he had walked around the corner of the bank and disappeared. She was angry with herself, and yet defending herself. She was throwing herself at a man's head, and he was ducking every lunge. Inside she heard Katie and Squint talking in low tones. Elliott was telling the nester's girl about the beauty of the trail, the emptiness of the country they passed through, and the glories of the Tall T ranch, which stretched from one river to another and embraced more acres than a mere man could estimate.

Dr. Dorris came by and gave his patient a swift examination. "I'm wasting my time with you," he said in disgust. "You're gonna live."

"Wal," Squint comforted him, "mebbe you can kill the next man, Doc."

The old man stopped on the porch with Grace. "He's a first-rate hombre," he said. "A girl like you oughta be looking after her own interests instead of giving Katie a clear field."

"He was Katie's from the start, doctor," Grace smiled. "You'll have to find me another man."

"I kill 'em legitimate like," snapped the doctor. "I don't marry 'em off. I try to give 'em a painless passing."

Then he was gone. She started inside but changed her mind. Every night and every day this place was getting more and more repulsive to her. Her uncle coughed in his room, and then she heard his faltering footsteps going out by the front entrance. Down to Fatty's, of course. Luther Coleman had to drink out another night.

She heard the clatter of boots on the board walk and waited hopefully. But it wasn't Brad. Cherry Carr turned the corner of the building and came toward her with his easy pantherish walk. Moonlight struck him in the face as he stopped at the gate, and she saw that his usual grin was missing. His lips were set in straight lines, and he seemed to be rocking back and forth on his heels.

"Miss Grace?"

"Yes," she said curtly, and walked to the gate. If Cherry had any notions of sparking her, she would slap those out of his head.

He came closer. She looked at him in a dull wonder, for

the moment forgetting her usual resentment of his insolent manner.

"This ain't my idea," he said thickly. She could smell whisky on his breath. "I do things different."

"What isn't your idea?" she demanded, regaining the frostiness with which she always treated him.

"This," he snapped.

Before she could guess his intent he had seized her roughly. She struck back instinctively, but the blow was wasted: hands seized her from behind and she realized in sudden terror that two other men were wrestling with her, and that Cherry's arm around her shoulders was squeezing the breath out of her. The two other men had run out of the shadows as soon as Cherry laid hands on her.

Something brushed her face—a soiled kerchief, which reeked of sweat and liquor, and was pushed into her mouth by rough hands while another kerchief completed the gag. When she tried to break free of Cherry's grip, his hands on her wrists tightened until she imagined she heard her wrist bones snap. She moaned and swayed in his grip. He caught her to him now, holding her head against his shoulder, and one of the other men tied her hands.

"As I say," Cherry muttered in her ear, "this ain't my idea. And nobody is gonna hurt you. Take it easy."

He picked her up as if she were a sack of grain and held her back in the shadows as footsteps were heard along the street.

Two men passed. Newt Norton was demanding: "Hunter, when are you gonna lay your cards on the table?" And Brad's answering quip floated back: "This is all draw, marshal. No stud. We'll have a showdown when everybody has made their draw. I don't mind saying I'm holding a kicker."

They passed on, and Grace Coleman's hopes sank. She felt Cherry, who was still holding her tightly, suck in his breath.

"Close call there," muttered the redhead.

Now he swung her over his shoulder. Horses were tethered behind the blacksmith's shop, in the same mesquites where Squint Elliott had hidden, and had drawn Grace's fire.

"Better lemme take her," said one of the other riders. Grace saw his face as he turned: it was a Sloping S hand called Pinto Eddie, with an uneven mustache and a violent temper. "My horse can carry double better than yours."

"I'll handle her," Cherry Carr snapped.

For some reason Grace Coleman was glad of this. She had her fears of Cherry, and her dislike. But these were nothing compared to what she felt for riders like Pinto Eddie.

Cherry held her in front of him on the saddle, his fingers biting into her flesh with the force of his grip. Then she was dizzy from the gait of his horse, off into a gallop at the touch of his spurs. She had never seen him do anything but run a horse.

The rain that had been threatening all evening was close at hand now, coming out of the mountains with the rush that valley people had come to expect. Here a change of weather came with stunning swiftness. One moment it was bright moonlight, the next dark and cloudy. With the second tier of cloud banks arrived the rain. The wind turned until it was out of the north, coming down in one boisterous chilling sweep, and the darkness was a solid wall all around them. She wondered how they were keeping to the road in this blackness.

This was the pass road, for they were climbing. Cherry

kept her face against his sweaty shirt, and she had to squirm to keep her nostrils free. The men turned off the trail, along a cattle path, and she knew they were riding away from the Sloping S headquarters and higher up on the rim. Evidently their plans had been made in advance, for there was no exchange of speech.

Now the rain hit in full force. Cherry swore softly and, holding her with one hand, fumbled behind him for his slicker. He unrolled it without slowing his horse's gait and held it over her head; but even so water began to drip onto her hair, and the wind, striking that wetness, set up a quick cold ache in her head.

Now they were out of the flat lands and in the scrawny timber which grew along the lower slopes. She tried to keep her sense of direction sharp, but presently it was as if she had been whirled around in a lightless chamber, the four quarters of the world blurring.

She heard Cherry speak once, to the men who rode behind.

"Keep up," he snarled. "Ed will kill us if this doesn't go off."

"Hell, there ain't nobody trailing us," grumbled Pinto Eddie. Not all men liked to ride their horses at breakneck speed through such blackness.

She was relieved to learn that they were abducting her on Ed Martin's orders. She hoped they were carrying her to Martin. She had no fear of the Sloping S owner, only a cold dislike. It was Cherry who held her quivering in apprehension—Cherry and Pinto Eddie. The redhead's ideas about women were known all over the valley; he had flaunted those notions boldly, and had gotten by with it. Ed Martin's reputation was none too savory—he was known as Ramona's admirer; but he would not lay a hand on her.

She believed she might be able to fight Pinto Eddie off. Cherry was the one she feared.

It was perhaps an hour later that they made a last turn and stopped. Cherry said, "We're getting down," and handed her over to Pinto Eddie, who let his hands linger on her, and rove over her, while he set her on her feet. She saw the leer on the man's face and yearned to have her hands free.

Cherry caught her shoulder, again forgetting in his excitement the strength of his fingers, and pushed her toward a shapeless black mass in the drizzle. Pinto Eddie went ahead and kicked open the cabin door, and she stepped into cold close air.

"Kick up a fire," Cherry growled.

"Hell, it's July!" answered Pinto.

"It's cold anyhow. The gal is shivering. We don't want her to get sick on us."

Boots scuffed around the cabin. A match flared up, blooming quickly in the heavy darkness, and Pinto cursed as he burned his fingers trying to light a lantern. The wick caught on the next match, and by the eerie flickering glow Grace saw that the cabin was unfurnished except for a sheet-iron stove, a battered long table and a board shelf hanging unsteadily to the wall. There were no bunks, and the floor was of hard packed dirt. Except for a pack of cards and an empty tobacco can, the table was bare.

Cherry caught her and turned her around with the same roughness. He jerked off the gag and said coldly: "Now yell all you want to."

Grace did not yell. For a moment the red-haired man stood watching her, the florid color of his face deepening and a look coming into his eyes that confirmed her fears.

Now there was a fire in the stove. Its warmth was welcome, for the quick hard-driving rain, whipped along by gusts of wind, had brought an unseasonal coolness to the cabin. She was shivering, and Cherry waved her to the fire.

"I can handle her myself from here on," he told Pinto Eddie and the other Sloping S rider, a gaunt stoop-shouldered man called Cherokee Charley, so called because he had at least one-eighth Cherokee strain. His Indian heritage showed only in his cheekbones and eyes, giving him a villainous look. Grace had heard Shadrock gossip that Cherokee was one of the worst men in the Sloping S outfit; but the man had always been polite to her, and she knew by his stolid impassive face that he intended no harm. It was the leering Pinto Eddie and the harsh Cherry that she feared.

"Ride on back, and let Ed know we got her," Cherry ordered. "You'll find him at Ramona's."

Pinto was disappointed. "Can't Cherokee handle that by hisself?"

"No," the redhead snapped. "You heard me, Pinto."

Eddie grumbled under his breath but followed Cherokee out of the cabin.

Grace Coleman took a deep breath. She was alone with Cherry Carr! She did not want to look at him; but, somehow, she couldn't avoid it. She turned her head, cautiously at first. He was holding out his hands to the blaze, his gaze upon her.

"Cold as hell—for July," he grinned.

But it wasn't the same grin she had noted before. And the eyes above his mouth were hard and calculating.

"Funny, ain't it?" he drawled. "You never gave me a tumble before. Always looked at me as if I was dust under your feet. Now you'll spend a little time in this cabin with me. Cozy, ain't it?"

"What do you want with me?" she demanded hoarsely.

Cherry noticed that her hand went to her throat and that her eyes widened in fright. He grinned again. So, at last, she was afraid of him. Cherry Carr had found that necessary to success with women; they must know him for what he was, be afraid of him for it, and yet unable to hold him back. That Katie Kimberlin, for instance, she had not wanted him. She had taken his caresses all cold and tense, as if any kind of motion, even to resist, was impossible, as if he had the eyes of a snake, paralyzing a victim with their bright intent glare.

"Oh, I dunno," he said carelessly. "Ed wants to talk to your uncle Luke about you. Said to keep you up here until he saw Luke Coleman and got what he wanted."

"What is that?" she demanded.

"Ed seems to think your uncle is trying to play games with him," the redhead shrugged. "Something about a double-cross on a deed."

Grace fought to suppress her fear. A woman who was afraid of Cherry Carr could never control him.

For a moment neither spoke. His bright eyes studied her from head to foot. Then, with a quick parting of his lips, he reached for the shelf behind the stove.

"A cup of coffee would go good in this wet."

"Yes," she said faintly, "it would."

Chapter Ten

THE HALF-BREED WOMAN broke in on Ramona as she was fixing her hair. Though Jeanne was her only girl, Ramona still exacted the same consideration and privacy: she was not to be disturbed by the average patron, and a man who asked for her had to send his name. Then, if she chose to receive him, it was in the small reception room, which retained some of its former splendor while the other rooms in the two-story house were going to rack and ruin.

"Ed Martin's outside," said Jeanne. "Wanna see him?"

Ramona frowned. Ed was a creature of habit; it wasn't like him to be coming into town for an evening this early in the week.

"Yes, let him come in," she granted. "He can wait until I've finished my hair."

She would have been as lordly with any man, perhaps even Drifting Dan Thompson. Many men, some of them important as far as wealth and position were concerned, had cooled their heels in her reception room while she completed her toilette. Her kind of woman had a ceaseless fight with an enemy who gave no quarter—old age. Few held their own as well as Ramona.

Ed Martin thought that as he stood up when she entered the reception room. She had never had a visitor who didn't pay her this respect. Jeanne and the other girls (when there had been other girls) were sometimes tossed around by playful customers. Never Ramona. A man returned her quiet dignity, even a man like Ed Martin.

"Dang it, Mona," he said, "you get purtier every day!"

He reached for her possessively, but she thrust off his hands with irritation. Men sometimes overplayed their part in this association between them that had never been anything but business and never would be. Ed Martin in particular had presumed, for there was no reason why she should like the Sloping S owner, and many, many reasons to the contrary.

"You're in town a lot these days," Ramona said, sitting on the stool before him. Jeanne had already brought him a drink, and she could tell that it had not been his first.

"Yeah," Martin said unhappily. He gave her a moment's study. Even a man like him could weary of loneliness. Even a man who was going beyond the pale of the law could yearn for someone to share his worries. "A guy is trying to put the skids under me," he grunted. "Another is slipping me a double-cross. I got to fight one off and settle with the other."

Ramona smiled. She knew this broad-shouldered, dark-faced man. He was a dangerous creature and yet a simple one. He was a menace because he sometimes carried out the geometrical axiom that a straight line is the shortest path between two given points. He was simple because he made up his mind to follow a course, and never thought beyond the conclusion of that immediate scheme. Brad Hunter had come to see her again, and had told her of recovering his money.

Usually she felt a loyalty toward her men; and she had a genius for steering between their hates and their prejudices. It took diplomacy to hold the attentions of Newt Norton and Ed Martin through twenty-five years, when one held the other in quiet loathing and for months had stalked his trail hoping for an excuse to kill. She had done this.

But also this young Texan had rekindled a spark which had burned delicately, but everlastingly. She had sent Drifting Dan riding away, but the memory of Drifting Dan was here again; and this lean drawling young man had been a son of Drifting Dan, and was the personification of the son she and Dan might have had together had they ridden a different ridge in the years when neither was old enough to bear the responsibility of laying out a trail. (No other loyalty can stand up alongside this one, for this is a woman's life, except when it is only a kind of life, as Ramona's had been.)

As she looked at Ed Martin her lips curved in a smile, and she gloried in the way she held him in the hollow of her hand.

"So Luke Coleman double-crossed you? What has he done with the deed?"

He started. "What do you know about that?"

"Everything," she smiled. "Luke also comes here."

Coleman did come, but very seldom in recent years. He no longer had interest in Ramona or any other woman, in anything but drinking himself into insensibility.

"The little rat! He should know better than to try and pull a shenanigan on me."

"Knowing you," Ramona murmured, "I'm sure you're taking steps already to get even."

"I got his gal." Ed Martin beamed with pride. "Cherry carried her up to one of our line cabins tonight."

Ramona gasped. She knew Cherry, of course. But not as she knew other valley men. The redhead had no use for her house. "Hell!" he had sneered. "I don't have to buy mine." He had teased Jeanne roughly, but that was all.

"Luke will come across, or his gal will pay," Ed said grimly. "He has to have her. He'll cough up the deed, and then I'll kick his teeth in."

Ramona nodded. Ed Martin would. But she could not feel sorry for Luther Coleman. He came to her house and blubbered of his dead wife. Even a woman like Ramona had her pride. No woman wanted to be told that she merely satisfied the desires another woman had kindled.

There was a hardness about this dark-eyed woman who had lived a lifetime here in a Wyoming town that had flamed up, and then had died. There had to be. She studied Ed through half-closed eyes as he leaned forward and caught her shoulder in a rough grip. Let him torture Coleman. There was a debt due, and the banker had not paid it all. And, as she endured Martin's pawing fingers, she smiled in anticipation of the time when life would throw in its grim, certain foreclosure on Ed Martin, the man who had separated her and Drifting Dan Thompson.

Luther Coleman was lost without Grace. Throughout the morning he tried to conduct the business of both bank and store; but his whisky-sodden brain did not function as of old. He could not make change, and he could not remember the prices of items. By midafternoon he locked the front door and rolled toward Fatty's.

Early that morning Pinto had ridden up and had aroused Luther with much shaking and cursing.

"Word from Ed Martin," the rider had snapped. "Don't worry about your niece until tonight. Don't squeal to Newt Norton. If you do, you'll be sorry."

"Grace!"

"Yeah. Ed will see you tonight."

And Pinto had spun off, leaving the startled liquor-doped

Coleman to piece together the rest of the story. Grace was gone, and Catherine Kimberlin was alarmed. She had told Squint, and the Texan offered to send for Brad Hunter and turn the responsibility of the search over to the Tall T owner. But Luke did not want this. Pinto had brought him Ed Martin's threat, and he was afraid.

"She's just off visiting, I reckon," he said lamely. "Wait till tonight, and then if we don't hear from her . . ."

But he shook his head. A day was a long time to leave his niece in the clutches of Ed Martin's Sloping S crew. He had no idea what Ed Martin wanted. He had already agreed to swear there was a deed to the Sloping S on deposit at his bank; but, as he had pointed out to Ed, there was nothing he could do if the court demanded that the paper be produced. Certainly it was something about the deed, and he shuddered. Martin would go to any length to protect his claim on that ranch, as he had resorted to violence to get it. Nothing but whisky would ease Luther's torment.

He bought a bottle at the saloon and returned to his room. Sloping S men were drifting in and out of Fatty's, and there was Newt Norton watching everything with his wise eyes, and he wanted to be away from them. He stumbled back to his house just before sundown and pulled the door of his room shut behind him and took one deep drink after another. He was a coward for not riding straight to the Sloping S and demanding his niece, and he knew it. Once he would have done just that, and no man's hand would have stopped him, only a man's gun; but now he was merely the wreck of a man, both physically and spiritually —and he knew that too.

Squint Elliott and Catherine Kimberlin were grateful for the closed door. Squint now was past his nightly fever and had little real need for Katie's attentions; but she stayed close to him, eyes brighter than ever. She made hot coffee at his request and broiled a steak in fresh country butter. He downed a huge meal, finishing just as Dr. Dorris came by for his daily visit.

"I ain't wasting any more of my time on a waddy who can eat like that," snapped the physician, a twinkle in his eyes.

"Gimme a shot of whisky, and I'm ready to ride," declared Squint. "Seen that boss of mine hanging around? The danged guy ain't been in all day."

"No." Dr. Dorris turned to Katie. "You're staying here against my advice," he warned. "Don't get within arm's reach of this crazy galoot. He ain't sick any more, and you might as well go home."

"Get out of here, and tend to your pill rolling," yelled Squint.

The doctor retreated with a chuckle. Squint looked up at Catherine with alarmed eyes. "You ain't believing that quack, are you?" he demanded. "I can't get around very well yet. You gotta stay until this leg of mine is set for travel."

"I'll stay," Katie answered coyly, "until my mother sends for me. Or Mr. Hunter tells me to leave."

"Call him Brad. He don't like mistering."

"Yes, Mr. Squint."

"And lay off that 'mister' in my direction."

"Yes, Squint."

Katie Kimberlin turned away to hide her blushing. How different was this man from masterful scoffing Cherry Carr! She shuddered at the memory of Cherry's hands, rough and compelling, and his breath hot and damp on her cheek. A thousand times she had regretted her meeting with the red-haired cowboy in the willows. Cherry had possessed a physical attraction for her, as for every woman; but Katie knew now that her submission had been physical only, that Cherry Carr had meant nothing to her and never would mean anything.

As she prepared supper she thought about Squint with a quickening of her heartbeat and a tremble of her hands. What would Squint think of her if he knew about Cherry? Living in a pine-hidden nester's cabin, never meeting on even terms boys and girls of her own age, Catherine knew little of what men thought. She had heard talk of marriage, and had thought of marriage, of course, but only in a re-signed manner, as of something impersonal, something not even appealing. For what was there about the only marriage she knew to tinge a girl's cheeks and eyes with stardust? Maude and Calvin Kimberlin had lived together a lifetime, that was all.

She did not realize it, but she had yielded to Cherry be-cause of this life of hers, if it was a life. The Kimberlins had never sighted a group of Sloping S riders without shivering with fear. That Calvin Kimberlin had lived on in Sloping S country after Bill Bradley's murder, knowing full well that he was hated by Ed Martin and also held in some fear because of what he knew about that night when the Sloping S had been set afire and its owner killed, spoke eloquently of the nester's mute yet timid stubbornness. Nothing about this country was more fatalistic, not even the creatures of the wild. Calvin Kimberlin had built his cabin here, and here he would stay until driven out by brute force. Mean-while he must turn off the trail when Sloping S men rode toward him, and he must never come face to face with Ed Martin, reminding the Sloping S owner with his pres-ence that homesteaders still slunk through his pine woods and furtively cast their seeds in his spring-streaked valleys.

What chance, then, had this homesteader's daughter against the Sloping S foreman, who had the demanding arrogance of a cattleman with a nester, the assurance of a man who had met and conquered life with a girl who had never known it, and was approaching its threshold with nothing behind her but the narrow emptiness of the life Calvin Kimberlin had led?

These things Katie Kimberlin thought—in mute bitterness. If she had done wrong in yielding to Cherry Carr, it was because of others, and she was not to blame. She had heard that dark things happened to girls who knew men out of wedlock. Their lives were considered to be ruined, and men did not look upon them except in an indecent way; and for them there were never marriage and children and homes, in the way women want them.

She looked back at Squint Elliott. The man was silently appraising her. Until she knew Cherry Carr, she had not been able to evaluate a man's attention. Now she could note a difference between the way Cherry had spoken to her and looked at her, and Squint's gaze. It was the difference rather than the similarity which embarrassed her.

The afternoon sun was retreating sullenly over the pass, hurling back last defiant shimmering rays of light. Katie turned into the kitchen again and started washing the dishes.

Squint called to her through the door: "A woman like you belongs in Texas. You're wasted in Wyoming."

She bent her head to hide the redness in her cheeks. Perhaps he was only teasing, as all men teased, even those who went no further than talk. She thought again of Cherry Carr, and shuddered. She pictured the cabin in the hidden valley, and saw again its barrenness, its discomforts.

And she knew, in a sudden bold decision, that she wasn't going back to it. For two days she had gloried in the possessions of Luther Coleman's niece—the dishes, the tablecloths, the rugs, the beds, the sheets, the thousand things that to a woman make life worth living. She was grown; one man had taken her, another wanted her.

She rolled up the dishrag and took off her apron. She walked back into Squint's room and stood over him.

"Then," she demanded, "why don't you take me back to Texas with you?"

Now it was Squint's turn to redden. Now it was his mind which was a whirlpool of confusion. He raked her face with his quick questioning look, and he knew that she meant what she had said. Her gaze was level and intent, and she had lost much of her shyness in this sudden cannon of thought which had made her a different woman in the twinkling of an eye. In such a fleeting interval a girl becomes a woman, and men from then on are never their masters.

"You danged little critter," murmured Squint, "you mean that."

"Of course I mean it," she answered promptly.

Then she saw his indecision, and the force of her mood was gone. She turned back into the kitchen and picked up her apron.

Behind her Squint rolled a cigarette. "Dang her hide," he whispered to himself, "she means it!"

Instead of washing the dishes, however, Katie Kimberlin pulled a chair up to the sink and buried her face in her hands. Why had she said such a crazy thing! Could Squint Elliott think anything more of her than Cherry Carr had thought? With one she had been an easy mark, following his tug, surrendering meekly to his force. With the other she had been brazen and forward, throwing herself at his head. The awful thought entered her head that Squint might be married already.

She heard Luther Coleman stirring in the other bedroom. In a moment he came into the kitchen, his eyes bloodshot and his lips trembling.

"Any more of that coffee, gal? And I could sure use a mite of soup."

She got both for him while he sat on a stool and regarded her with unseeing eyes. His fixed gaze made her tremble. Until liquor had soothed his nerves, he was always a fearful sight. His white hair gave him an ageless look, and its unkemptness a wild one. He did not even see her as an individual. In recent years he had lost track of people's identity. It did not occur to him to ask why she was in his house, doing the work his niece had always done.

He sipped his coffee slowly, then forced himself to eat the soup. He was not hungry, but he dimly recalled that he had not eaten this day, and that the aching inside might well be from starvation. After eating he staggered outside and sat on the front porch. Katie asked if she could bring him anything else; but he shook his head, not bothering to thank her for the solicitude.

Katie sighed. She did not know enough of drink to hold a man who had succumbed to it in scorn. Calvin Kimberlin had never permitted liquor on his place, nor had he ever touched a drop in town. Thus she could not reason that Luther Coleman was reaping what he had sowed. She pitied him, and wished she could give him some information about his niece's whereabouts. But he had not mentioned Grace except to mutter that she must be all right, and that her prolonged unexplained absence was no cause for concern.

Darkness dripped down from the pass in heavy drops,

one after another, and Katie returned to her patient. She lit a lamp and produced a deck of battered cards at his request and pretended to be absorbed in running cold hands of stud poker. Patiently Squint tried to explain the evaluation of his hands, and they played for matches; but when she turned over five hearts as too weak to challenge his pair of kings he gave up with a grin.

"Reckon," he murmured, "I'll have to do the poker playing in this family."

She was thrilled by the casualness of his talk, and his use of the word "family." She raised her eyes to his, though it seemed to her that leaden weights lay upon her lids, and that they were immovable.

"It's a man's place," she murmured, "to do the poker playing."

Maude Kimberlin would have thrown a fit if Calvin had ever looked as if he wanted to get into a poker game. But Katie would not treat a husband as Maude had treated Calvin, nor tolerate such treatment as Calvin had given to her mother. Nothing she had seen, of a concrete nature, had changed her belief that life did not have to be humdrum, and that marriage did not have to be a grim, pleasureless duty; but of a sudden she was filled with calm anticipation, and could look upon this man with confidence and smugness. He saw the look in her eyes and exploded.

"Dang it, you don't know a blamed thing about me!" he stormed. "For all you know I may have a dozen squaws back in Texas. I may be wanted for rustling and stealing hosses besides."

Katie giggled. "You talk so silly, Squint," she said. Her moments of awe and timidity were passed.

Squint Elliott sighed. And then he grinned. "Gal," he declared, "I ain't got a chance against you. But danged if I don't kick up my heels a little. Git out of here and let me sleep."

She obeyed with a chuckle, the indulgent little laugh women reserve for the men whose petty individual vices suddenly become appealing traits of personality. And then her face clouded and her lip trembled and the joyfulness of her mood left her as she remembered Cherry Carr. Did it take one such man to make a girl appreciate another man?

She slept on the porch, on the canvas cot where Luther Coleman was sitting; and she was too timid to ask him to leave his seat so that she could retire. In a half-hour he stumbled past her and into his own room, and she slipped off her dress and stretched out in the comfort of the night breeze trickling down from the hills. She could hear Squint tossing. He was a restless sleeper. She could hear the banker cough, and then the splash of water as he drank from the pail in the kitchen. She was afraid he would come back to the porch, but finally he returned to his room. Then she was sound asleep.

So was Squint. The sound of the Texan's snoring drifted to the banker as he sat on his bed and turned up his bottle. It was his second drink since eating, and it always took the second to set his blood to tingling and his senses to functioning. One was only enough to make him realize that liquor was what he needed.

A third, and quick. The thought of Grace in Ed Martin's power haunted him. Luther knew from sad, bitter experience how ruthless Martin could be. He dreaded the moment when Martin would come to see him. He had a fear of the man, a fear that had grown into an obsession. For a long time he had nourished it, and it was this fear rather than his conscience which had made him what he was. Fear of Ed

Martin had moved him to make his proposal that they divide up the Sloping S ranch and dissolve their partnership. Ed had swindled him on that division beyond a doubt. Luther had known it then. Then, twenty-three years ago, he had first faced the problem of this fear. He had evaded it—physically. Mentally it had never disappeared.

Now he must face Ed Martin again, Ed and his threats and his coarser superior strength. He eyed the shot-gun hanging above his door. It had been a long time since he had taken his gun and demanded his rights as a man.

Until Ed Martin had faced him and stared him down, he had held his own. Ed had made a coward out of him. And a drunken derelict. Ed was responsible for the death of his wife, who had wilted rapidly after learning how her husband had secured his start in Shadrock, how he had lent his sheriff's authority to the deliberate murder of a man, and the seizing of the man's ranch.

He drank again, and drifted off into the quick, unnatural sleep of a man who has drunk too much. As he slept he moaned from the pain of his unnatural dreams.

He must have slept that way an hour or more, with not a sound echoing through the open house except the rumble of Squint Elliott's snoring and the murmur of Katie's deep breathing. He slept in his liquor-laden soddenness until midnight came, and Ed Martin left Ramona's to tether his horse behind the deserted blacksmith's shop across the street from the banker's side door.

Earlier in the evening, in the saloon downing drink after drink, Ed had been conscious of Newt Norton's glance, and the cautious, discreet interest of men who had hitherto taken his presence in town as a matter of course. He had come into Shadrock half expecting to find a hue and cry over Grace Coleman; he had been relieved to realize that her disappearance was not generally known, that evidently the banker had followed orders.

He crossed the street on his tiptoes, fearing that Newt would round the corner and ask questions. He knocked gently, and then realized that Katie Kimberlin was asleep on the porch. The lamp was still burning in Luther's inside room, and he stole past the sleeping girl and the snoring Squint. He hesitated, and then rapped lightly at the banker's door. Getting no answer, he pushed it open and saw him asleep in the easy-chair.

With a grin he shut the door, then shook Coleman roughly.

"Wake up, Luke. It's me, Martin."

The shaking and the rough whisper penetrated Coleman's dreamland. He awoke, and reached for his bottle with a shudder. The shudder became a convulsion as he saw Ed Martin over him, grinning evilly.

"I want that deed, Luke. I want it right now."

"What deed?" whispered the banker thickly.

"The deed to the Sloping S. The Texan put it on deposit with you against the day he files legal claim. You snitched and put in this paper."

The ranchman shoved the paper with its scrawling print under Luther Coleman's eyes. He read it at a glance, and his face turned ashy gray in fright.

"Honest, I didn't, Ed," he babbled. "I never touched the safe. My niece put that deed in there. I didn't touch it, honest."

"You've lied to me before, Luke Coleman. You've holed up here like a slinking hound pup for twenty-three years, figgering how you could get even with me. This chance to double-cross me came, and you grabbed it. You don't get by with it, Luke. I got your niece, and I'm keeping her until you come across with that deed."

"Ed, for God's sake, don't hurt that girl! She's all I got left. You took most of the Sloping S, and you left me—"

"Damn you, don't accuse me of gypping you," Ed flared. "I dealt square with you, and you know it."

"You crooked me."

Ed drew back his big hand. "Don't say that again, Luke," he threatened, the purpose of his visit lost sight of in the rush of his anger. He hated this white-haired, drunken derelict. A man so helpless had no right to make such accusations.

The banker pulled back. Falling out of his chair as he turned, he landed in a sitting position against the bed. There he crouched, eyes terrified, lips moving speechlessly, while Ed Martin walked around the bed and stood over him, grinning and gloating.

"You always were afraid of me, Luke. You always knew I was the better man. Now get that deed, and don't gimme any more backtalk. I ain't got time to fool around."

"I haven't got a deed."

Ed's answer to this repeated denial was to slap the banker's face roughly. "Now are you getting me that deed?" he panted.

Coleman cringed to the floor.

Martin kicked him. "Damn you, Coleman," growled the dark-bearded man, "I'll stomp you to death. Git moving. Git me that deed."

Coleman rolled to his feet. His eyes looked around the room wildly and came to rest on the shotgun hanging over the door. He dived for it. Ed Martin guessed his intent.

"Don't, Luke. Damn you, don't—"

But now the banker had the gun and was turning with it. Ed Martin jerked at his revolver and shot quickly as the barrel of the shotgun came up, but it was impossible to miss at that range. He pressed the trigger again, and Luther Coleman slumped against the wall, the shotgun dropping from his hand.

"Don't, Ed," murmured the banker. "Don't."

Then he slumped forward and fell sprawling, arms out at full length. Ed pushed his body aside with his boot toe and gave the room a quick glance. Perhaps the deed was here, in Coleman's desk. He jerked open a drawer and spilled its contents over the floor.

Squint Elliott's voice startled him. In his anger he had forgotten that people must have heard his shooting and would come running.

Ed Martin wheeled and fired in the same motion. Squint, standing in the doorway, threw himself back when he turned; but he was not quick enough. The slug tore into his shoulder.

Martin now heard Catherine's bare feet pattering across the kitchen floor and voices outside shouting inquiry and trying to locate the gunshots. He hesitated, gave the desk a yearning look; then dived through the open window, tearing away part of the sash with his elbow and cutting his wrist on the glass pane. He landed on his hunched shoulders and leaped up running.

A shadow was racing around the corner of the building. He recognized the marshal and threw a quick shot at him. As the bullet whistled close Newt Norton withdrew behind the bank. Ed raced across the street and to his horse tethered in the mesquites. Twice lead whistled by him. But he bent low in his saddle and spurred his horse into a dead run and knew he was clear. It would take time for a pursuit to form.

Newt would have to go back to the livery stable for a horse. In that time he could be lost in the darkness.

Newt realized this and, before going back to the hotel, ran into the house. He helped the tearful Catherine Kimberlin lift Squint Elliott and carry him back to his bed. Squint's shoulder oozed blood, and his lips were tight from the pain of this new wound.

"Winged again," he sighed.

A .45 slug leaves more of a wound than a ball of buckshot.

"Go git the doctor," Newt snapped at Katie.

She ran out in her nightdress, frightened to tears. Her lips moved as she raced toward the frame cottage where Doc Dorris was already stirring.

"All right, all right," he grumbled as she pounded on his door. "I'm coming, I'm coming. Who is it now? A man never gets a decent night's sleep in this town."

Already Newt Norton was studying the wreckage of the banker's room. Coleman was dead, and Newt's lips were tight. This was murder, and in his town. He came back to Elliott's bed.

"Gawdamighty," murmured the Texan, "this is some country. Twice I get shot when I ain't doing anything but standing around. I'm heading back to Texas where things are peaceable."

The marshal's lips quirked, tempted to break into a smile. "You got the luck of the damned. Just a flesh wound. Who was it? It looked like Martin, but I couldn't swear it in court. He got away so fast."

"Is Coleman dead?" Squint counterquestioned.

"Yes."

"Poor old guy!" sighed the Tall T foreman. "He couldn't have put up much of a fight."

"A man sooner or later gets what is coming to him," Newt said harshly. "For a long time Luke Coleman got by."

"I heard 'em," murmured Squint, "but at first I thought I was dreaming. What did Martin want to kill him for?"

"You'll swear under oath it was Martin?"

"Sure, sure. Saw him plain as day. You don't get an ugly mug like his mixed up with anybody's."

Newt nodded. There could be no mistake. This was Ed Martin's brutal work. "I've been waiting for that a long time," he murmured.

His gnarled hand patted the butt of his gleaming gun. "A long time," he repeated. "Twenty-five years. I wished at the time Bill Bradley had been killed where I was the law."

He started toward the door, but his exit was blocked by Catherine and Dr. Dorris.

"Newt, can't you keep order in this town?" demanded the physician. "There hasn't been so much shooting since the boom days."

"Business is picking up," Norton admitted.

Catherine darted by them, suddenly aware of the thinness of her cotton nightgown. Newt turned away and then stopped as he heard hoofbeats. The horse galloped up, and its rider rolled out of the saddle, almost falling. Newt cursed softly and ran out to give a hand.

His eyes widened in surprise.

It was Grace Coleman.

Chapter Eleven

As THE CLATTER of Pinto's and Cherokee's horses died away, Cherry Carr rolled a cigarette. His sardonic eyes flitted over Grace's face and body. He did not conceal the fact that he was amused by her fear.

"Funny, ain't it?" he grinned. "You never would touch me with a ten-foot pole. But here you're staying out in a line cabin with me. For one night anyhow."

There was an insinuation, as well as a triumph, in his tone. Both were deliberate.

"If you lay a hand on me, I'll kill you," Grace told him hotly. He did not know it, but the attitude that had worked with so many other women had given her new life. Angry blood stained her face until it was darker than her tawny bronze-swept hair. She had never thought of herself as a strong-spirited girl before, but she knew now that if Cherry harmed her she would be able to kill him with her own hands. In this Cherry had misjudged her; he had estimated that fright would weaken her, as it did most women.

The redhead chuckled. "Reckon you'll get to liking me," he drawled confidently.

He ground out the cigarette under the heel of his boot, standing up. Then, deliberately, catlike, he moved toward her.

She stood up to meet him, face grim, lips working furiously, but not whimpering.

"I ain't gonna hurt you," he grinned. He sat down at

the table in the other rickety chair and looked up at her. "My lap here is a good place to sit."

With a motion as deliberate as his walk, and as tense as his eyes, Grace slapped him.

He took the blow with a smile. "Like to see a little spirit," he drawled. He reached for her and pulled her down on his lap. He was quick with his motion; he caught her unprepared.

But only for a moment. He wasn't holding her hands. She brought both sets of fingernails down his flushed face.

Blood leaped there as Cherry swore. "You little hellcat!" he snarled. "I'll show you what a man is like."

Now, as he caught her closer to him, wrestling with her arms, he was rough, and his gloating grin was gone. She fought him silently, with none of the sickening fear she had felt before. He tried to carry her to the dirty bunk; she twisted free of him and kicked viciously as he lunged at her.

It was a short chase. The cabin was small and the red-head's long arms seized her.

"By God, you're a handful!" he panted.

Now he increased the pressure of his arms. His was the superior strength; she began to weaken. She realized her waning force with the same fear that had made her power-less before. Now it lent ferocity to her defenses. She clawed again. And bit. As her teeth closed painfully on his wrist he slapped her hard with his free hand.

It was a painful blow. Her head rang from its force. Suddenly she didn't have the strength to fight any more.

"I'm—all—out. You—win, Cherry."

He reached for her hungrily, and she couldn't resist him. His lips were tight and hard against hers, and his whiskers scraped her cheeks. She could not avoid his kisses, but no one of them, nor all of them, moved her. Nor the caresses of his fleeting hands, experienced in thrilling women. There was nothing but cold loathing in her face and eyes, and he suddenly, surprisingly, stood up, letting her drop down on the bunk.

"I believe," he murmured, "you mean it."

He lurched over to the table, rolled a smoke, and struck a match. As he looked back, the grin returned to his carrot-shaded face. "You're a stubborn critter," he chuckled. "Too stubborn for me."

She couldn't believe the sudden freedom of her arms, the lack of a pushing weight against her shoulders, the absence of a straining, panting breath against hers. She lay limp and stared at him with eyes that didn't dare to believe.

"Cherry, you mean—" she faltered.

"Hell, yes!" he shrugged. "All fillies fight a little—a man comes to expect that; but, if that's the way you feel about Cherry Cart, I ain't bothering you."

Tears leaped into her eyes. She had not dared hope for this. She, also, had underestimated a character.

"I guess," Cherry mused, "I shouldn't have hit you. But I got a prejudice against biting. No woman ever bit me before."

Grace Coleman rolled over on her face and wept.

"Dang it," growled the redhead, "turn off the water-works. Nobody was gonna hurt you. It never hurts any woman to love a man. We're made for it. All of us."

"But you hurt and—I—was scared and—"

"Of course you were scared," he said in disgust. "Women always are. Having a man is something they're afraid of. But they can't do without 'em. I can't figger out women. A man, now, tries to satisfy his tastes. My kind of man anyhow. I like a drink when I'm thirsty and a steak when

I'm hollow inside. I don't go for this notion that there's just one woman in the world for a man. Or just one man for a woman. We all feel about the same to a horse."

She stopped crying. She looked up, suddenly hating no longer, suddenly seeing him as she should have realized he was from the first, a man riding hell-for-leather on trails he chose on the spur of the moment, and riding each one to its end.

"You're not all bad, Cherry," she said softly. "Some day you'll find the right woman. When she gets through with you, you'll be a fine person."

"Don't reckon any woman will ever put a halter on me," he shrugged. "I ride 'em high, wide, and handsome. Now I'm gonna sleep."

And he lay down on the bunk where recently they had fought. He showed no concern for her welfare. She waited until his deep breathing assured her he was asleep, then gently tried the door. She had not noticed that he had locked it, but the redhead had made sure his prisoner would not escape. The only window was over her head and was not large enough for her to struggle through if she could have reached it.

Then she tossed her head with some of Cherry's devil-may-care philosophy. She eyed him enviously, then lay down on the floor. Cherry, she told herself, had the manners of an Indian—calmly appropriating the only bunk and leaving his prisoner to sleep on the floor.

Her sleep was uncomfortable, restless. She awoke an hour before dawn, cold from the dirt floor's dampness, and kindled a fire. Cherry rolled awake with the first crackling of the flames. He had no question as to how she had passed the night. He looked on the cobwebby shelves and cursed when he found no food.

"I'll have to ride to the ranch after grub," he said. "I'll be back about noon."

"Leave me some water, please."

The redhead found an empty coffee can and filled it for her from the near-by creek. "This will have to do," he shrugged. "Nothing else."

"I would say," smiled Grace, "that you aren't fixed up to entertain visitors, Cherry."

Just like that, the psychological advantage can change between man and woman. Grace Coleman would never be afraid of Cherry Carr again. From now on she could match his lighthearted carelessness.

"The last one," grinned the Sloping S foreman, "didn't complain."

She heard him whistling as he swung into the saddle after making sure the door was locked behind him, then the clatter of his horse breaking into a swift gallop.

The hours dragged until he returned with beans, cold bacon, stale bread, and coffee. Manlike, he had forgotten sugar and a pot, but Grace managed with their water can. Cherry ate glumly, then retreated outside. She lay on the bunk and slept again. Now the chill of the rain had passed, and it was warm. Here in the cabin, with the door firmly locked, it was hot and stifling. She called to Cherry, hoping to persuade him to trust her outside, but just then she heard him riding off. He didn't return until after dark, and then he was in a glum mood.

"Dang this sitting around!" he complained. "This ain't no job for old Cherry. I'll trot up to the headquarters and get somebody to sit in for me."

Grace paled. Another Sloping S rider might not have the decency she had found in Cherry. Another rider might not care how hard she fought, or how long.

"Please don't," she begged. "Cherry, what have you brought me out here for? I'm not bothering Ed Martin surely. I just work in my uncle's store and bank. Why kidnap me and hold me out here forever?"

"Well," he said hesitantly, "I reckon we did rush into it. Ed brought it up, and I jumped at the chance. I had a notion that, if I ever got you alone, you would see things my way."

"Why did Ed want me kidnaped?"

"Your uncle is trying to double-cross him," the redhead drawled. "Remember that deed the Texan deposited with you? Luke Coleman snitched it and substituted a piece of paper."

"No, he didn't."

"Somebody did," Cherry shrugged.

"My uncle did not touch that piece of paper," Grace avowed. "I'm willing to swear to it. He ran out of the bank looking for Ed Martin as soon as I told him that Mr. Hunter had deposited ten thousand dollars and a deed with us."

Cherry studied her. "You're sure of that?"

"Positive."

"Did you see the deed when the Texan handed it to you?"

"Why, no. It was an envelope in his wallet. I counted the money, of course. And witnessed the markings."

"Markings! The ten grand was marked!"

"Yes."

"Gawdamighty!" murmured Cherry. He was silent a moment, then his lips creased in a mirthless smile. "Ed and me really jumped off the dead end," he mused. "Ed especially."

Then he remembered something. "Me, too," he said cheerfully. "I guess I got a kidnaping rap to face."

"Not necessarily," Grace said with sudden decision. "Take me back now, Cherry, and I'll never testify against you or bring charges against you. You haven't harmed me. Nobody will ever prosecute you for what you've done."

He thought this over. The idea appealed to him instantly; she could tell that by the brightening of his eyes. "Mebbe you've got something there," he murmured.

"It's the only way out, Cherry," she urged.

"I'll do it," he agreed. "Besides, I got to find Ed and set him straight. He's got a temper, you know, and he's also a one-track mind. He's plumb set on the notion that your uncle is trying to pull the wool over his eyes. We'd better ride."

Grace felt suddenly weak. This ordeal was over. Cherry was taking her back to Shadrock unharmed.

The redhead opened the door but went out first, leaving her to follow. He rolled into his saddle, leaving her to untether the horse, and then to swing up in front of him. Certainly, she mused, Cherry wouldn't take a prize for gallantry.

It was a wild ride. Cherry's thoughts were far ahead, and he held her with such a looseness that a thousand times she was afraid of falling. But, by some miracle, she held on, and then there were the dark shadows of a Shadrock that was asleep in front of them. Cherry rode to the front of the bank and let her slide down.

"You oughta sleep better tonight," he chuckled.

Then they noticed the light in the home behind the bank and heard the excitement.

"Gawdamighty!" exclaimed Cherry, and spun his horse around.

Grace ran into the house, past Newt Norton without a word, and into the room where Dr. Dorris was bandaging

Squint's shoulder while Catherine Kimberlin watched anxiously.

Newt came back and caught her shoulder. "Easy, honey," murmured the marshal.

"What is it, Newt?" she demanded. "Is Uncle Luke—"

The lawman nodded. "Dead. Ed Martin killed him."

"Is he—in there?" she asked in a quivering voice, pointing to the bedroom.

"Yes."

"I'll go see him," she said resolutely.

She closed the door behind her. Catherine Kimberlin started in, but Newt Norton checked her.

"Let her alone. She's got some talking with herself to do. She'll be all right."

Then he spun out of the house. Ed Martin was now within the range of his particular law. No need to wait for Sam Dugan to act. Ed Martin had killed a man in his town.

He dressed hurriedly and ordered his horse. He asked at the hotel and found there were only two men asleep there who could be deputized. He roused Maggie and Chuckling Charley, despite their vehement protests, and pressed them into service.

"Never thought," grumbled Maggie, "I'd be woke up at two o'clock in the morning and made a deputy marshal."

"Why don't law men work in the daytime?" Charley wanted to know.

Newt did not heed their protests. Too busy with his own thoughts. Ed Martin would certainly ride straight to his ranch. But it was unlikely he would stay there. Then where? He should throw up a dragnet around the valley, certainly should guard the pass. He needed more men for that.

He carried his two new deputies toward the Texan camp.

This was a man hunt Brad Hunter would surely want to join in; and the marshal could use some of the Tall T riders.

The trio was challenged five hundred yards from the Tall T wagons by Brad himself, who was taking a night trick.

Norton explained what had happened. "Your man just got winged," he said. "Got more lives than a cat."

"Tough to kill," Brad nodded.

There was a grin around the young Texan's lips. "I guess," Newt added gently, "that you figured Martin would plug Coleman? Or did you hope it would be vice versa?"

"I didn't care," Brad answered calmly.

"One of 'em is out of the way," Newt murmured. "Saddle up your horse and pick out some of your best boys, and we'll go get the other one. I figured you would want to be in on the kill."

"No," Brad snapped. "Make up your posse of Wyoming men, marshal. We're sitting this hand out."

"What!" Newt could hardly believe his own ears. The son of Bill Bradley was being offered a chance to hunt down the murderer of his father, and was refusing!

"Dang it, Hunter," sputtered the law man, shaken out of his usual somber calmness, "I gotta have help. I ain't afraid of Martin man to man, but combing these flats is risky business. He can shoot straight, and he's desperate."

"I know that," Brad admitted; "but my men and me— we're not getting in this Wyoming war. Deal us out."

"Wyoming war, hell! Look, Hunter, I've given you rope. I could have made things uncomfortable about that bank robbery deal. Inside, I've been backing your play. This is the showdown, and it's time to lay your cards on the table. Luke Coleman is dead. Ed Martin is wanted for murder, and this time a crooked sheriff can't stop the rap. Ed will face a jury if he gets taken alive. What's wrong with you?"

Brad didn't answer.

The marshal snapped: "I've seen you run from Martin twice. You're careful never to have a gun around when trouble is brewing up. Are you just plain yellow!"

He sensed the trembling in Brad Hunter's lean body, and wondered if he had gone too far, and if Hunter would turn upon him, who wanted to be the Texan's friend and ally.

But no, Brad regained control of himself. "It's not a question of being yellow," he answered tonelessly. "It's a question of this ain't our country, and Coleman's murder ain't our responsibility."

"But your foreman was shot up!"

"Accident, I reckon. We'll leave it lie, Marshal."

Newt shook his head regretfully. More than wanting man power for his posse, he had wanted to ride side by side with the son of Bill Bradley and the protégé of Drifting Dan Thompson in a hunt to the death for Ed Martin.

"Have it your own way," he growled. He had his pride. He wouldn't beg any man's help. If he had to go after Martin alone, he would go alone.

The law man turned away and climbed into his saddle. "Ready, boys?" he demanded of Charley and Maggie. His voice dripped with what he thought.

Brad turned back to the campfire. Pecos joined him there, thoughtful and moody. There was leftover coffee. They warmed it.

"You know, Brad," murmured Campbell, "the boys heard some of that powwow."

"I reckon they did," was the curt answer.

"They ain't proud of you, Brad. It ain't a Texan's way to dodge a fight, specially when one of our boys has been shot. They set a heap by Squint Elliott. They've ridden rivers with him, and they don't like sitting out here cooling their heels when there is work to be done."

"They have their orders," Brad said grimly. "The first man to put on a gun and mix up in this is fired."

Pecos sighed and pushed back the brim of his hat. "Then some of 'em are gonna want their time, Brad," he said sorrowfully. "Me, I'm sticking. I don't know what the deal is, but I'll ride with you."

"Anybody can have their time who wants it," Brad repeated. "Any of 'em. All of 'em."

Pecos studied the lean grim face half visible in the thin wavering firelight. "What's up, son?" he asked gently.

"I'm just playing my hand, Pecos," Brad answered in a softer vein. "Talk to the boys, will you? Tell 'em not to get ants in their pants."

"I'll try," shrugged Pecos, "but I know some of 'em are ready to pull out. They know you're after this Sloping S outfit. Why, Brad? What could you do with it if you latched on to it? You got the best grass in Texas."

"I don't know," Brad sighed.

"Then ain't you been to a lot of trouble to get something you ain't sure you want?"

Brad nodded. He thought of Grace Coleman, and sighed again. His scheming had led to her uncle's murder. That would always stand between them. She would never see that Luther Coleman should have been killed, and that a man had to pay his debts, regardless of a woman who stood in between. His lips tightened. The chips would have to fall where they would. The ambition of a lifetime could not be thrust aside. Newt Norton was right; the showdown was here.

"Day after tomorrow," he said, standing up, "we move in on the Sloping S, lock, stock, and barrel."

"That's the talk," beamed Pecos. "The boys will follow you right up to the corral gate, Brad son. And there ain't enough gunslingers in all of Wyoming to hold us back."

Chapter Twelve

SQUINT SLEPT a long time. His new wound had brought a weakness, but Dr. Dorris swore it was a clean hole and there was no danger of infection. Probably the Texan wouldn't even be feverish as from the buckshot.

"I wish the galoot would go on back to Texas," grumbled the physician. "I've worked my fingers to the bone ever since these waddies rode in here."

Katie took her post by the bedside, determined to be there when Squint awakened. Twice the wounded man called gently for water, drank it without ever completely awakening. Then, just before noon, he stirred and opened his eyelids. He saw her by his bed and grinned. He reached for her hand and squeezed it gently.

"I was scared you'd check out while I was asleep," he murmured.

"No," she whispered. She had sat by his bedside for hours, and most of that time had been spent in earnest thought. She had reached a decision. She feared its aftermath, but it was only right.

"Still going back to Texas with me?" Squint asked.

"Do you want me?"

"Hell, I ain't making all this palaver over nothing."

Katie took her hand from under his. "I want to tell you something first," she said unhappily.

"Yeah."

"It'll probably make a difference in—the way you feel."

"I doubt that," he said gravely.

"There was—another man. Once."

There, she had said it. She couldn't meet his questioning glance.

"I know what that means to a man," Katie whispered, her head low. "I didn't love him. I don't know how it happened. It just—did."

Now she raised her glance, defiant, expectant. There was a fleeting movement of Squint Elliott's lips, and then he closed his eyes.

"I didn't hear you, Katie," he whispered.

"I said there was—"

"Don't talk, Katie," he broke in. "I feel weak again. I guess I need another nap."

For a long time he lay there with his eyes closed, and she thought he was sleeping. Then he raised himself up on his elbows, and she knew that he had been deceiving her all along.

"What was his name, Katie?" he asked gently. "Or don't you want to tell me?"

"Why not?" she answered bitterly. It was as she had feared. A man couldn't forget, or forgive. "It was Cherry Carr."

"That redhead!" growled Squint. He caught her hand again. "Cherry and me will have a little talk when I get up. You and I got nothing more to say about it. Have we?"

"I haven't," Katie blurted. "Mr. Squint, you're—gosh—you're the—"

"Forget that 'mister,'" he snapped. "And why don't you kiss a man? Don't you know how?"

"No," Katie murmured truthfully, bending toward him, "but I can learn."

Brad sent Dollar Bill over to the Sloping S ranch. "Tell the boys that Ed Martin has killed Luke Coleman and is on the run. Tell 'em I got proof that I'm Bill Bradley's son, and I'm taking over the outfit tomorrow afternoon. I don't want any of 'em there. Their boss has fanned the breeze, and they got nothing to fight for. Tell 'em to pull out."

Dollar Bill nodded. This would make sense to the men who had ridden for Ed Martin.

The Tall T owner went to the wagon where Jinx Duval was held a prisoner.

"I'll give you a break," he said grimly. "Your boss is washed up in this country. Your outfit is through. Make a deposition that you robbed the bank on Martin's orders, and I'll give you a running start. Right now Newt Norton is busy chasing Martin, and he'll probably never get around to bothering about you."

"That's a deal," Duval nodded.

He couldn't write, but could affix a crude signature. "I want another witness," Brad said. "Not of my own outfit. Ride into town with me and we'll get another party to attest your signature."

"Town," Duval said nervously, "might be dangerous."

"I reckon not. You can take my word that nobody will bother you."

He and Jinx rode to Fatty's, and the oversized bartender agreed to be a witness.

"Reckon," Brad said, "you don't need to know what Jinx here is signing for a while? He overplayed his hand, and he's leaving this country right pronto."

Fatty nodded. A barkeep learns sympathy for men who sometimes have to leave a territory right unexpected. He watched Jinx scrawl his name on the paper a second time. Brad took it from Duval's fingers and handed it to the salon man.

"Better keep this until Newt turns up," he said. "You can vouch, then, that I haven't changed the document in any way."

"Sure," Fatty agreed. He studied Duval's face. "You knew what you were signing, Jinx?"

"Bueno," nodded Jinx. He took a deep breath. This wouldn't be the first country he had ridden away from. "I'll buy a drink, Hunter," he proposed.

Brad hesitated, then nodded. "Here's to you and the Sloping S," murmured Duval. "I'm glad a good man is going to get it."

"Luck to you, Duval," the Texan answered.

Jinx downed his whisky and then slouched through the door without looking back. Brad drank another.

"Heard from Norton?" he asked Fatty. He knew that saloon men kept up with everything.

"Trailed Martin as far as the pass," nodded the barkeep. "Evidently Ed got away into the badlands. If so, nobody will find him."

"Norton will get him," Brad said grimly. "Newt will get him. Newt will get him if he has to follow him to hell and back."

He walked around the corner and knocked hesitantly at the Coleman door. Grace herself answered. She had not shed many tears over the death of her uncle. It was horrible to think of Luther Coleman having been murdered, but she could console herself with the assurance that he would have drunk himself to death in a few months anyhow; and that

160

Luther, while fearing Ed Martin, had not hated the thought of dying.

She could tell herself that it was best Luther had died this way, abruptly, painlessly. As far as her own plans were concerned, she was glad to be free of his charge. An offer had already been made for the store, bank, and living quarters, and she intended to take it.

"Why, come in, Brad," she said, surprised that he had knocked. For a day or more he had ignored this formality.

"I won't bother you much," he said, his tone and manner aloof. "I'm here to offer my sympathies about your uncle. And to see Squint. I'd be glad to help you in any way I can."

He rattled off the words like a parrot, as if they had been rehearsed.

"Thanks. I can manage, though."

"I won't be running in and out like I have. You won't have to put up with that."

"That isn't an imposition."

Why should he think it was? How plain did a girl have to make things?

"We've bothered you too much already," he insisted.

He found Squint and Katie holding hands. The nester's girl reddened slightly as he entered, but made no effort to withdraw her hand.

"Dang your hide," grinned Brad at his foreman. "You'll be eating Limpy's chow in another week."

"No, Brad," Squint said soberly. "I'm pulling out on you."

"What!"

Squint grinned at the flushing Catherine. "Got me a gal, Brad. From now I'm riding double."

"You old son of a gun," murmured Brad. He sat on the

foot of the bed and rolled a smoke. "So she listened to you? Katie, that was a big mistake. Down in Texas nobody ever paid any attention to a thing he said. The only way to handle him."

"Thanks, friend," Squint chuckled. "Knew you'd give me a jump."

"Just warning the girl," shrugged Brad. "She can still back out."

"I'm sure," Katie said positively, "that I don't want to, Mr. Hunter."

"Call me Brad. But look, podner," he said to Squint, "you can't pull out on me just because you're getting hitched. The Tall T could stand a woman around."

"When a man gets married," insisted Squint, "he's gotta think about a spread of his own. I got a start, Brad. I reckon I've put off splitting up this long just because it was kinda—"

His voice dropped off. He didn't know how to put his thoughts into words.

"I know, you flop-eared waddy," Brad grinned. "But you don't have to go so far. There's land around us. Reckon we've covered more with our cows than we gotta have. You can latch on to some of it, and we can be neighbors. Pool our stuff in the spring roundup."

"Sure, sure."

Then Squint remembered something. "Katie, would you mind letting us powwow by ourselves?"

The girl promptly left the room. Squint pulled himself up on his elbows.

"Podner," he said anxiously, "you gotta handle a guy for old Squint. Me, I won't do any shooting for a long time. And this galoot certainly needs a shot of lead in his intestines."

"Who is it?" Brad demanded.

"This redhead. Cherry Carr."

Hunter frowned. Cherry had tossed challenging hints his way, but he had found them easy to overlook. Cherry's type of man never infuriated him.

"Carr? Why, Squint?"

"Reckon, Brad," was the gentle answer, "that's a question I can't answer. You gotta take my word for it."

"That ain't hard to do," agreed Hunter. "I sent word to the Sloping S boys to clear out. We're moving in tomorrow, cattle and all."

"Dang it, and I'll miss the fight," sighed Squint.

"There won't be a fight," Brad denied. "Ed Martin is on the run with Newt Norton on his tail. Cherry may stand up and bark back, but the rest are probably over the hill by now. They got nothing to stay and fight for."

"What about the legal side of it?" Squint demanded. "Can you get by with just moving in?"

"I'm working on that today," Brad said. "Filing claim to the Sloping S and the flats around the creek mouth. Don't expect trouble. I'll have to get Maude Kimberlin in to swear I'm Bill Bradley's son, I guess, but that's all."

"What are you gonna do with the ranch after you get it?" Squint asked. "Podner, you can't stay in this country. Texas is in your blood, and—"

"I know it," Brad sighed. "I kinda looked on this as a picnic. Settling some old scores and running into some excitement. Now that I got it, I don't know I ever wanted it. Drifting Dan could see that. He never would let me come while he was alive. Then he made me promise on his death-bed that I wouldn't start shooting, that I wouldn't try to settle up with a gun."

Through the open door he saw Grace Coleman busy

with dinner. "A man ought to take the trails as they come, Squint," he murmured.

"Yeah," nodded Squint. He laid a hand on Brad's arm. "About that redhead? Mebbe he flew the coop. Mebbe he didn't. If you get a chance—"

"Me and him will have a talk," Hunter nodded.

He stood up and put on his hat. Grace called from the kitchen.

"Stay for dinner, Brad. No more trouble to cook for four than for three."

"No," he said crisply. "Gotta be riding. Thanks anyhow."

Grace did not press the invitation, but, as soon as he had ridden off, she came to Squint.

"Is there any chance," she demanded frostily, "of persuading your friend that I'm not poison?"

"Reckon Brad never had that notion," the foreman answered gently. "Things are on his mind, and he has gotta do some talking to himself. If I were you I'd sit tight."

"I suppose," she said slowly, "that he is afraid I will hold a grudge—"

"Yes," Squint interrupted. "And he packs a mite of one himself. He ain't the type of man you can crowd."

"No," sighed Grace, "he isn't."

Ed Martin rode at a gallop toward the Sloping S ranch, his head cooling and his lips working. He didn't regret killing Luther Coleman; he wasn't the man to spend time regretting anything. It had happened, and now his anger had cooled and he could start scheming how to make the best of the situation before him.

He hadn't killed the Texan, not that this mattered. There was plenty of proof available that he had killed Coleman.

This would be called murder by a jury. A cattle country jury doesn't always consider a range-war killing in that light. There had been mutterings when Bill Bradley had died, but no open agitation to arrest the ringleaders. Things like that were part of a cow country's make-up.

But now—Ed Martin knew full well that he had lost one fight. He had to clear out of this country, and that meant leaving the Sloping S ranch to the first man who moved in on it. That would be the Texan, of course. This Brad Hunter would step forward and make his play, and nobody would be there to challenge him.

Martin reached the ranch and hurriedly made a roll of blankets, extra socks, a clean shirt, and a handful of grub. Newt Norton would be on his trail, and he realized he had better grab what start he had. He didn't even leave a note for Cherry Carr, or awaken any of the boys sleeping in the bunkhouse. To hell with them! Let them shift for themselves.

They would scatter when they learned he was gone. Perhaps they might hang on for a while, hoping he would come back, but not for long. He wasn't coming back.

He had no choice. He had no fear for most men; but for years he had been conscious of Newt Norton's sustained hostility. He could still remember the marshal's cold rage at Bill Bradley's death, and his growling offer to lay aside his law man's star and shoot it out man to man.

Martin had no particular fear of Brad Hunter, or of any posse that Newt might organize. But Newt was a different matter. Once Shadrock had taken the diminutive marshal too lightly. That was when Drifting Dan Thompson had been the country's deadliest killer, the fastest man with a gun in all of Wyoming. Ed had seen that fight himself.

Thompson blandly self-confident, grinning at this marshal who was little more than a kid. Ed had dived out of the way, like every other startled but thrilled man in Shadrock, while the two gunmen walked slowly toward each other; and the Shadrock people had been shocked to see the kid law man walking right on at his regular pace, giving Thompson all the break there was.

Those watching had known when Drifting Dan was ready. They had seen it in the famous gunman's face and eyes. They had seen his hand dip, and they had shivered at the roaring. Then, as the smoke curled away, they had seen Dan Thompson in the dust on his knees, clutching his shoulder, and Newt Norton coming forward to take the gunman to jail for a crime no more serious than breaking up a few chairs in Fatty's saloon. And Dan Thompson, whose trail other Wyoming law men had carefully avoided, served out his full thirty days!

When Newt Norton unlocked the jail door, he handed Thompson his gun. But Dan had done an about face and had become a law-abiding man. Newt had become his close friend. Martin had seen them more than once. Every Saturday night Newt had taken a corner table in Fatty's and ordered whisky and two glasses and waited patiently, never for very long, until Drifting Dan came in. Until, of course, that Saturday night when Dan didn't come, and, instead, talk floated in of the burning of Bill Bradley's house and of the death of Dan Thompson in a running gun fight.

Perhaps, but for Newt, Ed Martin would have stayed and fought it out; but, with Newt on his trail, he had to travel, and travel light. He galloped away from the ranch and toward the pass. Morning came rolling over the summit, and he saw the three men behind him, Newt and Charley and Maggie. Ed sought the rocky ridges where his horse would not leave a trail. Once he stopped for a smoke and to think things out.

He couldn't go far without money or grub. If he followed the road over the pass and toward Fort Laramie, he would run into a hornet's nest of pursuers. If he left the trail and took the badlands route, he would be on his own for a long time, too long. Ed Martin was a cunning man when his temper was not flaming. He spurred his pinto down the ledges of the high rim and went sliding to the bottom of the first cliffs. Then, dipping lower, he cut back toward Shadrock, swimming the river a mile from the Texan camp, riding stealthily through the brakes across the stream. He approached Shadrock cautiously, waiting for night to drop. He ate what grub he had and rolled up the last of his tobacco. Then, as darkness came, he swam the river again and approached Ramona's from the rear, leaving his horse by the river bank and going from tree to tree.

He had seen from his hiding place that he had thrown Newt off the trail. The marshal hadn't been able to follow him across the rocky ridges. He would spend the night at Ramona's, and the following day. She could buy shells for him and grub and get money that he would need when he had crossed the badlands.

He didn't dare risk the front door but tapped lightly on the window of her reception room. She was alone, and admitted him promptly.

"I thought you would come here," she whispered.

"You've saved my skin, Mona," he grunted.

Chapter Thirteen

ED MARTIN OUTLINED what he wanted over his drink. Ramona listened calmly. She nodded. Yes, she would help him make his get-away. Ed fell to complaining of the bad luck that had been riding him, and she recalled other wanted men who had made her house a temporary hide-out, and who had stolen away reequipped through her generosity. Drifting Dan Thompson had followed her from Dodge City to Shadrock. And here, in this very room, Drifting Dan had had his wounds dressed and had slept while Ramona herself had rocked to sleep a tearful little boy who couldn't understand what was happening to him and his world. A woman like Ramona has so many memories.

She brought Ed another drink. He would stay there that night, he said. And the next day. The volunteer posse would by then have spent its energies, and he would only have Newt to contend with. Getting away under darkness, knowing the trails, he could get out of the valley and into the badlands before daylight. Once there, he challenged any man to hold his trail.

Ramona returned to the kitchen. Jeanne was sulking from the lack of trade; the half-breed girl would not be here very long. She had already served notice she was going on to Fort Laramie where there were soldiers.

"Jeanne, I want you to do something for me," said Ramona.

"Hell, I'm not a servant," snapped the girl. Her kind was miserable when there were no men around.

"Go to Newt Norton's hotel and tell him Ed Martin is in my house."

"Say, you ain't double-crossing your best customer! Martin has spent more money with you than this marshal ever will."

"Newt has never spent a dime and never will," snapped Ramona. "But do as I say."

"Sure, if you wanna be a chump," shrugged Jeanne. "Now I know I'm pulling out. I don't wanna be mixed up with a madam who will pull a stunt like that."

She pulled on her light coat, though the night was warm, and walked along the path with a bold whistle. She had protested, but Ed Martin's welfare meant nothing to her. All men were suckers and should be played as such. Maybe, she mused, Ramona was in love with that sour-faced Newt Norton. If so, it served her right.

Norton's voice startled her. The law man slipped out of the cottonwoods and caught her shoulder, whispering, "It's all right, don't yell."

"Say, give a gal warning!" protested Jeanne. "You scared the daylights out of me sneaking up on me like that."

"Who's in the house?" demanded Newt. "Is Martin?"

"Yeah. Just blew in. Ramona sent me to tell you."

"Ramona sent you?"

"Sure. I told her Ed Martin had spent enough money with her to get an even break, but she has gone loco."

"It doesn't matter," Newt said tonelessly. "I had a hunch he would show up here. Ed is too clever to strike the badlands as light as he was."

He gave the girl a shove. "Go on back," he said. "Act as if nothing had happened. I'll be along in a minute."

Jeanne obeyed, slipping back into the house. Inside Ramona's room Ed Martin was still drinking. Ramona was being generous with her best whisky. She held this man in some scorn, but she did not underestimate his physical powers. Nor his bravery when backed into a corner. Newt Norton would not arrest Ed Martin without a fight. The more Ed drank before Newt came, the more unsteady and the slower would be his aim.

Ed pawed her as she sat before him on the stool. "Come with me, Ramona," he urged. "I'll get out of Wyoming and send for you. There is a boom in Nevada. We can pick out a wide-open mining town and rake in the chips. I'll set you up in a house like you've never seen before. I tell you what, I'll even marry you!"

That was a generous offer—from Ed's viewpoint. Ramona's lips twisted. Men offered her a wedding ring with such obvious magnanimity. As if she would take any man in return for a valueless legitimacy.

"No, Ed," she declined. "Thanks, anyhow."

"Why not?" he demanded. "What's left for you in this valley? I'm pulling out and—"

She laughed gently. Men, men! How quickly they could assume that a woman was dependent upon them! She had lived before Ed Martin came; she would live after he had gone.

"What's here for you, Ed Martin?"

The voice came from behind him. Ramona herself had not heard Newt Norton's approach. Noiselessly the marshal had pushed aside the curtains and opened the French doors. Now he stood framed in the lamplight, cold eyes upon Ed Martin, arms crooked at the elbows, shoulders pointing forward.

"Norton!"

It was a gasp, a frightened, shocked gasp. Ed Martin leaped up and made a motion at his gun.

"Think it over, Ed," Newt rasped. "Hold it right there. I'd rather shoot it out with you than carry you in; but I'm a law man, and I'll accept your surrender."

"Like hell you will!" snarled Ed, rocking back and forth on his feet. His malignant glance turned to Ramona. "You double-crossing wench!" he snarled. "I trusted you. After the dough I've spent on you I thought you could deal straight."

Ramona Custer leaned forward. "Remember Dan Thompson, Ed Martin?" she asked in a fierce, low voice. "I loved him. You killed his friend and drove him away. He never came back. But *I'm* here, Ed Martin. I've been here this twenty-five years. And the friend of Dan Thompson is here, Newt Norton."

Ed scowled and cursed softly.

"Remember how Newt shot Dan down?" gloated Ramona. "We thought no man in Wyoming could outgun Drifting Dan. The breaks went against you, Ed Martin. Instead of facing Dan Thompson, you have Newt Norton. Newt is faster. Newt shoots straighter. Turn around, Ed Martin. Go for your gun. Newt is waiting."

Ed Martin hung back. "Newt, dammit, I ain't got a chance against you. Gimme a break. A horse under me, open country ahead. That's my game. Nobody ever could beat you on a quick draw. It's murder, that's what it is."

"Then drop your gun, and I'll take you to jail."

"To hang! Hell, no! Gimme a run, Newt. Five minutes."

"No."

Perspiration broke out on Ed's dark face. He glowered at Ramona. "Damn you," he whispered.

Then he jerked at his gun and turned with the same

motion. Newt Norton's hand moved simultaneously. There was a crashing report, and a picture which had hung on Ramona's wall for twenty-five years rocked unsteadily, and then dropped to the floor. Its glass frame splintered into a thousand pieces, flying all over the room.

For a moment Newt Norton did not speak. For a moment the marshal stared at his smoking gun barrel.

Then he looked up, and his lips parted. "We'll clean up the room, Ramona," he said gently. "I'll get him out of here, and you sweep up the glass. Then we'll have a drink."

"Yes," murmured the woman. "I need a drink."

Newt found Charley and Maggie at the saloon and beckoned to them. "My gawd, can't you let us alone?" wailed Maggie. "We just get rested up from one day's riding when you come after us again. We ain't going into the badlands."

"No need for it," Newt said. "Martin is dead. I need your help to pack his body out of Ramona's."

"That's different," said Cheerful Charley. "Ain't many men I'd rather help bury than Ed Martin. I'll even use the ignorant end of a shovel if you say so."

"Just help me get him to the courthouse," Newt declined.

The three of them lifted Martin and laid him across Newt's horse, then walked alongside their grim burden out of the cottonwoods and past the saloon.

There Cherry was standing, a crooked grin on his face. The redhead strolled out into the street and stopped the procession.

"So you got Ed?" he drawled.

Newt nodded. "Want his body?"

Cherry shook his head. "The county can bury him for

all I care. The outfit has broken up. That Texan sent 'em word, and they took off like a sage hen."

There was bitterness in his tone, and a challenge. Cherry seemed to have aged a little. His eyes were red as if he had lost sleep. But there was still the same insolent confidence about him.

"Did all three of you get him?" he demanded.

"No," the marshal answered shortly. "He had his chance. I always give a man his chance, Cherry."

Was there a challenge thrown back at Cherry Carr? For a moment the redhead thought there was.

"When a man starts looking for trouble, Newt," he growled, "he can always find it."

"Is there anything we should have trouble about, Cherry?" Norton asked quietly.

Carr shook his head. "No."

"If any of the boys are around," added Newt, "tell 'em to get out of town. Martin is dead, and the rightful owner of the Sloping S probably will claim his property."

"That would be this Brad Hunter?"

"Yes. Probably he packs proof that he is Bill Bradley's son."

Cherry's lips curled. "But he doesn't pack a gun. He lets you do his killing for him."

"Mebbe," murmured Norton, "he is smart in that. I get paid for it. So long, Cherry."

Cherry Carr rode back to the Sloping S and slept that night. The next morning he cooked his own breakfast, and then sat on the bunkhouse steps and smoked cigarette after cigarette. The Texans had said they were taking over today. Cherry knew it was foolish to even think of trying to keep them off, but he hated to see the Sloping S change hands without some kind of fight.

With a strange calmness he noted what an inglorious mess were the corrals, the barns, and the bunkhouse itself. The yard outside was littered with empty tin cans, some of them rusted to remnants, others with their bright lithographed labels still intact. The mud in the chinks of the log walls was dry and falling out, and wind-blown dust had accumulated on the floor.

Cherry had no regrets that Ed Martin's day at the Sloping S was over. He had never shown good ranching sense. Even with his riders slapping brands on anything they saw in the brush valleys, he hadn't prospered. Cherry, who had the instinct and pride of a ranchman, looked around at the disorder and sighed. He remembered what his father had said—that a ranch with warped corral fences wasn't making money. This Texan now, this Brad Hunter, would straighten out things in a hurry. Cherry liked the way the Tall T's wagons were painted and greased and the way the Texas riders kept their saddles and harnesses. Right now, as he stepped out of the bunkhouse, he had to wade through a litter of broken-down gear, rotting buckboard beds, piles of scrap iron, and mounds of rusted horseshoes.

Some of Ed Martin's horses were still in the corral, though most of the riders had left on his stock and even carried a spare. Cherry gave the horses a thoughtful study. They belonged to him as much as to anyone. As far as that was concerned, there was nothing to prevent him from rounding up the cattle on the pine-streaked slopes and grabbing himself a stake.

It was typical of Cherry that he shrugged this idea aside. He wanted no further part of the Sloping S. He sighed wistfully as he thought about Ed's handsome Spanish saddle; he could use that.

He walked back into the bunkhouse and filled his saddlebags with items from the pantry: dried venison, sugar, salt, beans, tobacco. He exchanged his rifle for a Winchester which Ed kept in the partitioned-off office but had never used. Ed's Sunday boots, he found, were just a half-size too large for him. Better than his own worn footgear. He rummaged further through Ed's things. Some shirts he could use. And socks.

Then, rolling a last smoke on the Sloping S bunkhouse steps, he looked around in unsentimental farewell. He would have fought the Texans to the death at a word from Ed Martin; but he was glad that the man was dead and the Texan would get the ranch. He could forgive Ed all his sins except being a poor manager with cattle.

Then he swung into the saddle and rode slowly toward the pass. He followed the trail through the pines that led to the edge of Kimberlin's, and grinned as he recalled the night by the spring, when Katie had yielded to him. At that, he had plenty of pleasant memories to carry with him out of this valley. He could regret, perhaps, that he had worked for the wrong man, but even that didn't worry him. It was high time for him to be riding a few more hills anyhow.

He was five miles from Shadrock, and starting up the pass trail, when he decided to gallop back to Fatty's for a farewell drink. He was not thirsty. His desire for a drink had nothing to do with it. But it had occurred to him that he could not ride off without one last gesture of defiance. Ed Martin had run, and had been killed on the run. The Sloping S outfit had scattered without a backward look.

But Cherry Carr was leaving just because he wanted to. And Shadrock might as well know it.

Curious eyes followed his progress down the dusty street until he rolled out of his saddle, flipped a smoke together and looked around in mild interrogation. Then no man met him face to face. Maggie sauntered by and nodded curtly.

Newt Norton left his perch on the courthouse steps and came toward the saloon.

"Howdy, Cherry," the marshal said pleasantly.

Cherry grinned. He knew what was bothering this town. They were afraid he would take up Ed Martin's fight. Even Newt was a little nervous over it, and had sauntered this way to give him his chance.

He didn't want it, of course. All he wanted was to make it plain that he was not afraid of it.

"Hanging around a spell, Cherry?" asked the law man.

"Nope," was the grinning answer. "Making tracks, Newt. Shaking the dust of Shadrock off my feet."

Sure he was. But he wasn't being chased out. He wasn't one of the Sloping S rats bolting away from a ship already sunk.

Newt nodded. "You're a good man with cattle," he said with studied carelessness. "You'll catch on somewhere. Luck to you."

Cherry hesitated. "Luck to you," he answered finally, as if with great effort. Then he pushed by Norton into the saloon.

Chuckling Charley was standing at the bar. Their glances clashed. Cherry's lips parted as he noticed that Charley pushed back his drink and turned until his back was squarely against the bar. This amused him, too. Charley had ridden with Newt Norton on Ed Martin's trail. But Cherry held no grudge.

The redhead took his drink and turned to study the handful of men inside Fatty's. Most of them were Jupiter's riders or town people, and all of them were watching him with quiet intentness. He gulped his drink, dropped a dol-

lar on the bar, and said loudly, "Keep the change, Fatty."
Now he could ride off without a backward look. He had
shown this town the color of his backbone.

He started out but was stopped by Charley. "The Texan,
this Brad Hunter," the now serious-faced bronc' peeler
murmured, "wants to see you. Probably knows you are
here now. One of his boys was posted here to watch for
you."

"Hunter!" sneered Cherry. "Run back, and tell him to
put on a gun and make man talk."

"He's got on a gun," nodded Charley. "Two of them."

Cherry raised his eyebrows. So there was to be a challenge, from the man he had least expected to make it. His
lips quirked. "Much obliged," he muttered, and stalked out.

He sensed the moment he stepped outside that something
was wrong. People were too tense. And, of a sudden, too
intent on staying in the shelter of the buildings and out of
the hot street. He bent his head to strike a match and light
the cigarette dangling from his lips. He took his time.

He didn't have to look up to see that Brad Hunter must
be stalking down the street. He could tell from the quietness
around him.

When he raised his glance he saw Hunter in front of the
bank. Coming slowly. Alone.

He noticed in that same roving look that the sidewalk
was suddenly clear. People had disappeared by magic into
doorways. Even the space in front of the saloon was wide
open. The only other person he saw in this quick darting
glance was Newt Norton. The marshal was back on the
courthouse steps, faded hat pushed back, face sphinxlike,
eyes narrow and considering.

Cherry grinned and tugged at his belt. It had been a long
time since he had played this part. Nobody in Wyoming

had ever done better. Except maybe Newt Norton. Cherry had his own ideas about that. He rolled toward his horse. He didn't know why Brad Hunter should come after him. The Texan had his ranch now, and ought to have sense enough not to start this futile, fatal fight. For he wouldn't walk away from it, not Brad Hunter.

With studied carelessness Cherry started to climb into his saddle. He knew what was coming, and that Hunter wouldn't stop, but he would let the Texan put the actual challenge into words.

"Carr?" called out Brad.

Cherry turned. Even acted as if he was surprised. "Looking for me, Hunter?"

"Yes. You got your gun, haven't you?"

"I always carry my gun," Cherry grinned.

He turned with this retort and started toward Brad, walking slowly. He wished it were a different man; a good cattleman like Hunter should live to put the Sloping S aright. But it would help him ride away from Sunrise Valley. It would give him another memory, and leave another behind.

"Whenever you like, Cherry," Brad called out.

Cherry nodded and came closer. He was enjoying this. This was what he had been raised to. He didn't want to get it over with all at once.

Now only thirty yards separated the two men. Now both stood stock-still, narrow glances hanging, tense hands alert.

Cherry moved first. He tugged for his holster, and someone screamed. It was the wife of a Shadrock man who shouldn't have been on the street at all.

The sudden crash resounded up and down the empty silent street. There were thin echoes shivering off into the open space beyond. There were eyes clamped shut in quick horror, then opened in undeniable, morbid eagerness.

And there, weaving back and forth, still grinning, was Cherry Carr. His gun lay in the dust at his feet. Again he wobbled. He went forward a step with the intuition of a fighting man. Even while dying Cherry Carr wouldn't step back.

He seemed to stumble, though there was nothing in the dust of this street to throw a man off balance. He reeled forward. They could see him fighting to regain his balance, and knew quickly, as he did, that he never would.

He slumped all at once, falling in a heap. Doggedly he tried to pull up to his knees. He couldn't. He sprawled there, half up, half down, his weight on his hands and knees.

The grin left his face. In its place came a look of mute questioning wonder.

He murmured something. No man could be sure what. Brad Hunter was closer than any, and Brad thought he said:

"What the hell, Hunter? What the hell?"

And then, with a sigh, he pitched forward on his face. Before he died, he smiled again. They buried him that way, a man still amused by the life he had led.

It took Shadrock a long moment to accept what they had seen. It took long moments for Brad Hunter to replace his gun in its holster and turn toward the saloon. But while other men watched with fascinated immobility, Newt Norton left the courthouse porch at a swift walk and was in front of the saloon waiting when Brad got there.

Newt held out his hand with a twinkle in his eyes. "Dan Thompson must have worked with you plenty, son. No man in Wyoming ever made a quicker draw."

Brad nodded. His eyes were strained, and his voice jerky. "That day you got Dan, he was—"

"I know," interrupted Newt with a nod. "Eyes had gone back on him. He got in the first shot and missed. I've always known that. But I figgered Dan wouldn't want it told."

"He didn't," Brad agreed.

Newt reached out and took Brad's gun. "Dan's?" he guessed.

"Yes."

The Texan hesitated. "He taught me," he said finally. "He spent hours with me. But Dan lived to be old enough to know six-gun law ain't much law. He made me promise that if I ever came back to Wyoming I wouldn't pull a gun to settle my grudges. He taught me a man should curb his gun hate, whether it's right or wrong. Cherry now was different. There was a reason, and it wasn't hate."

Newt Norton held out his hand. "My apologies," the marshal said slowly, "for what I've been thinking. The Sloping S is yours. Move in. I think you'll help out Wyoming."

Chapter Fourteen

MAUDE KIMBERLIN was washing when Pecos rode up to the clearing and asked her to come into Shadrock and identify Brad Hunter as the son of Bill Bradley.

She wiped her hands and regarded the full tub of soaking clothes ruefully.

"Couldn't it wait?" she demanded. "I could get this washing on the line before dark."

Hers had been an automatic protest, an unthinking gripe, spoken before she realized the import of Pecos' request. Now her face blanched, and her hands trembled as she took the washboard out of the tub and hung it on its nail.

Suddenly she was trembling and tearful. "Just a minute," she murmured, and walked away from the wondering Pecos into the cabin. There Calvin was stretched out on the bed. He had hurt his back trimming fence posts and wouldn't be on his feet for several days.

"Cal, Cal!" she sobbed. "What am I going to do?"

"What's the trouble, Maw?" asked her husband anxiously, rolling painfully to his feet. "Who is that man?"

"He's one of the Texas riders," blurted Maude. She sat at the hand-hewn table and buried her face in her hands. "This boy they call Brad Hunter is ready to claim the Sloping S. He's moving his crew into it today. They want me in town to identify him as Bill Bradley's son."

Her voice became a plaintive wail. "Cal, help me!" she cried. "What can I do?"

Calvin Kimberlin sighed. "I don't know," he whispered hoarsely. His gaunt face was gray with worry. "I knew you shouldn't have done it, Maude. I told you at the time you shouldn't."

"I know it, I know it," she sobbed. "But, Cal, I never thought it would—"

"It is in life," Cal said soberly, "that you pay for the sins which you in life commit. There is no turning back, Maude. You must reap what you have sown."

She stood up, wiping her hands on her faded dress, suddenly in possession of herself again. "It wasn't wrong," she said defiantly. "I did what any mother would have wanted. I'll go right in and tell them the truth."

She took a determined step toward the door. But this wasn't that easy. A woman simply couldn't decide what should be done, and proceed to do it.

She wilted again. "But, Cal, how can I face him and tell him that? It's nothing to tell a boy after all these years. Couldn't we just run away—or something?"

"No, Maw," Calvin sighed. "There's no running away. We got to look him in the eye with it, and hope he'll forgive us."

Maude Kimberlin reached up and took her wide-brimmed Sunday bonnet down off its peg. "He'll have to, Calvin," she whispered. "The good Lord will take care of that."

But the movement of her lips, in quick earnest prayer, showed that she was not so sure.

They were waiting for her in Norton's office: the sphinx-faced marshal, Brad Hunter, and Ernest Rogers, the Shadrock lawyer whom Brad had employed to represent him.

Not even Rogers was sure how this could be handled legally. There would be, said the attorney, the necessity of proving William Bradley was dead, which could be arranged by affidavits. There would have to be proof presented that this young man who called himself Brad Hunter was the son of William Bradley. Quicker and easier, advised the attorney, would be to declare the Sloping S open range and file a homestead claim. But Brad refused that.

The Texan leaped up as Maude came hesitantly into the room, twisting her gnarled hands, avoiding his smiling look.

"Thanks so much for coming, Mrs. Kimberlin," Brad said. "Here, have this chair."

She looked at him queerly, and her lips moved soundlessly. Then her glance dropped to the floor.

"Go get Judge Ross," Newt said to Rogers. The lawyer shortly returned with the magistrate.

"Judge, I'm not so sure about the procedure of such a case," Rogers said hesitantly. "As there is not a complaining party, perhaps you can advise. My client, who is known to us as Bradley Hunter, wishes to file claim to that land known around here as Sloping S ranch, occupied until today by Edward Martin. There not being a deed, we are going to have to—"

"There is a deed," Maude Kimberlin interrupted. She reached into the bosom of her dress and brought out a handful of worn papers. "Here is the deed. And Bill Bradley's will. I've nursed it all these years."

Newt Norton's lips moved in a mirthless smile. For years Ed Martin had tried to track down a deed to the Sloping S. All the time it had been within a short ride of his bunkhouse, in the custody of this woman.

"That will simplify matters," Rogers murmured.

Maude heaved a deep sigh. Then she stood up, on unsteady feet, her features twisted. "Before this goes on any further," she said, "I got some talk to make. I ain't ever told all about the night Bill Bradley was murdered and his house burned. I was scared to, with Ed Martin right there and the law never reaching out to protect us."

She paused for breath, and her eyes looked away from Brad Hunter.

"It's known in this valley that Juanita Bradley brought her young uns to my cabin," she went on tonelessly. "I had brought 'em into this world, and she turned to me as the only person she could trust. The poor thing was near death when she got there, from shock and fright and scarlet fever. She died the next morning. She never had a chance after seeing her husband shot down.

"There were the kids. My own two young uns were sick too, they had caught the fever from the Bradley kid a week before. Doc Dorris can remember it. He rode out to treat 'em, and he sat up all night with my little girl, who didn't live past morning."

Her voice fell off. She looked around her, but not directly at Brad Hunter.

"That night," she added in a hoarse whisper, "the Bradley boy died."

Somebody stirred in his chair. Newt Norton's face lost its leathery blankness. Amazement was written all over Brad Hunter's features.

"Yes, died," Maude Kimberlin insisted. "It wasn't the Bradley boy who rode away with Drifting Dan Thompson. Dan sneaked up to our cabin the next day. He was hurt but he had promised to look after Bill Bradley's son. He had ten thousand dollars in money and he aimed to carry the kid off to Texas and make a clean start."

Another pause. A pin dropping in this tense, quiet room would have made an awful clatter.

"I know I shouldn't have," Maude whimpered, fumbling with the buttons of her gingham dress, holding her head low. "But my own boy was just over the fever. He was

184

weak still, but I figgered he was well enough to ride. I sat there holding him in my arms and thinking about the life he would lead as the son of Maude and Calvin Kimberlin: kicked around; cussed at; half starved; never sure of a roof over his head; burned out; chased off one range onto another."

She raised her eyes pleadingly. She looked straight at Brad Hunter.

"Dan didn't know one boy from the other. Cal tried to stop me, but I wouldn't listen. Cal told me it wasn't right to give up my own flesh and blood. But it was easy, I tell you. When he rode away in Drifting Dan's arms, he was riding away from what Cal and Maude Kimberlin were. He was riding to a different country where he had the same chance as other boys. Drifting Dan didn't know, I tell you. He thought he was taking Bill Bradley's son with him to Texas —instead of mine."

Tears rolled down her cheeks. She dropped her eyes again.

"I kept the girl, Bill Bradley's girl. One of mine had died, and I had sent one away. Seemed like I should have one of the four. Cal and I couldn't stand living on alone."

She gulped. "You men want to know who owns the Sloping S ranch. Bill Bradley's girl does. Catherine Bradley. She's lived a long time as Catherine Kimberlin. I guess—I owe her—more than I can ever pay. I guess I'll hafta go down on my knees—and ask her—to forgive—a foolish old woman."

Not a man spoke for a long time. Then Brad Hunter said slowly, without turning: "I withdraw my claim, of course. My men have already moved in on the Sloping S. They are cleaning it up. They are putting my stockers out to graze. The place is a mess. There needs to be a new house. New fences. The two thousand stockers I brought from Texas will **give** the rightful owner a new start. In a few days, when things are straight out there, I'll take my men off. I'll take 'em back to Texas—where we belong."

His lawyer protested, "But this is merely one woman's story, Mr. Hunter. All the other evidence—"

"—doesn't amount to a damn," Brad finished for him. "Nobody can doubt she is telling the truth."

His lips quirked. "Least of all me."

Maude took a step toward him. "Son! My baby! Don't hate your old mother just because she's been a fool. She tried—"

"There is no question of hate," Brad interrupted. "It's a little hard to get used to, that's all." Then his tone took on a new gentleness. "But I can do it. There have been many times in the past twenty-five years when I wished I had a mother. There still are."

"You don't need to worry about us," Maude promised tearfully. "We won't bother you none. Go on back to Texas, and don't pay any attention to Cal and me. People don't even have to know about this. These gentlemen can keep a secret—like this. We'll live on till we die in our little cabin. You're a big man in Texas and—"

Brad Hunter laughed. His arm slipped around her, and she buried her head on his shoulder.

"You'll like Texas," he said softly. "The bluebonnets cover the hills in the spring, and the winter comes soft and easy. When it rains—"

Newt Norton stood up and cleared his throat. "I reckon," he muttered, "that I can stand for the drinks."

"Coming," said Judge Ross and Rogers in unison.

"You flop-eared galoot," growled Squint. "I was wondering if you were coming by to say 'So long.' I've been watching the pass all day. If you tried to sneak out on me, I was gonna run you down."

"Saved the best for the last," Brad grinned. "I sure made a deal up here. I get rid of the orneriest lyingest foreman in Texas. I betcha next spring we get more cattle out of the Nueces bottoms than we ever did before."

"Why, you ungrateful spalpeen!" roared Squint. "I done your thinking ever since Dan died. I've helped the place together."

"Aw, close your lip!" Brad said. He grinned again. "I'll tell 'em at the Longhorn that ol' Squint got up to Wyoming and latched on to an heiress; that he owns the best spread in Sunrise Valley and is making money hand over fist. They won't believe it, but I'll tell 'em."

"I wish, Brad," Catherine put in, "that you would take half the ranch; and, at least, let us sign a paper for the two thousand stockers."

He shrugged his shoulders. "It's worth it to get rid of Squint."

Catherine laughed softly and reached up and planted a light kiss on Brad's cheeks. A week of marriage, and the responsibility of planning her new home on the Sloping S, had brought out characteristics that her background had never given her a chance to express before. There was a new grace about her, and an assurance which became her.

"You liar," she murmured. "But I'll bring Squint to see you sometime."

"Sure," added her husband. "Mebbe we'll drive a herd of cattle to Ellsworth by way of Texas."

"Now I'll leave you tough-talking men to say goodbye to each other," Catherine smiled. "God ride with you, Brad. We'll never forget you."

"It goes double," he said huskily.

He climbed up on the fence as she returned to the house.

"You got a deal there, podner," he murmured. "You always were a fool for luck."

"Sure you ain't riding away too quick yourself?" questioned Squint. "This Coleman gal is all wool and a yard wide."

"What else is there?" shrugged Brad. "I brought about her uncle's death. Wouldn't that stand between us?"

"Oughta throw your loop anyhow," insisted Squint. "Once I did that at a roundup. Down in Webb County. We were roping for big dough. I figgered this dogie was long gone for the brush, but I threw my rope just the same. Caught both front legs and jerked in the prettiest underhanded catch you ever saw. Won me fifty bucks and jug of red-eye so strong it curled my whiskers."

Brad nodded. "Mebbe, Squint. But I gotta think things out. Guess I need some night watches. Things are happening so fast I— Well, it takes a little time to get used to all these—"

"Yeah, I know. I'll put in a good word for you, podner. I'll write you a letter. Mebbe I can tell you how you stand."

"Good."

Brad stood up, twirling his hat around in his hands. "Well, I'll be moseying," he said. "We'll be on the trail by noon. We'll miss you tonight, you ol' reprobate. The boys sent their best, and said to tell you it couldn't have happened to a better man."

"The same to them, dang their lazy hides," Squint muttered. "You gotta crack a whip over them waddies, Brad. They got it in them, but they're so danged ornery—"

"How much money do they owe you?"

"Not a thin dime," was the prompt answer. "I wouldn't lend one of them cheating sons a copper if—"

"They figgered it up last night," Brad interrupted. "Comes to a couple of hundred bucks, according to their calculations. Here it is."

Squint sighed. "I didn't expect a dime of it back."

Brad held out his hand. "So long, podner."

"So long," Squint said gruffly.

Brad rolled into his saddle, and Squint turned back to the porch. Catherine came out of the door and stood with him.

"Any chance," Squint growled, "of a man getting some hot coffee?"

"Sure," Catherine murmured.

Squint stood and watched. He could see the specks in the distance—the Tall T remuda. He sighed. The trail back to Texas. Rivers to cross and rough country to ride. Rainy nights with lightning flashing off a cow's horn. Soaked chuck in the dripping of a hastily sought shade. Steaks and pickles and coffee around a campfire. And the loneliness and beauty of starlit nights.

Catherine came back to the porch to tell him the coffee was hot. There were tears in his narrow eyes. She leaned against him.

"A woman has to do a lot for a man," she murmured, "to make up for what a man gives up."

"Some things," Squint sighed, "a man learns to get along without, and they don't make any difference. Some things a man misses forever."

"I know, dear," she whispered.

Brad Hunter now had reached the trail wagons. Traveling without cows, the remuda was haltered, and getting under way was an easy task. The wagons were loaded, and Limpy called he was ready, and Brad rode to the wagon where Maude and Calvin Kimberlin sat proudly, their eyes shining in anticipation of the trail ahead, and that trail's end.

"Ready?" he called.

"Wheel and deal," Cal Kimberlin answered.

Brad waved to Pecos, and the Tall T outfit started back toward Texas, where it belonged.

Its owner rode with Pecos, with the seventeen other hands strung out behind. No cattle to prod, no wings to ride. They would make time this day and every day.

But still they had to accommodate their pace to the speed of the wagons. It took a long time to reach the top of Sunrise Pass. Brad pulled up his horse and looked back at the valley, at the white speck which was the Sloping S headquarters, at the cluster of houses and the gray winding streak which was the town of Shadrock.

He wheeled his horse without warning. "I forgot something," he explained to Maude and Calvin. "Pick you up down the trail."

And he bolted back toward Shadrock.

His riders stared after him in mute wonder.

"There," murmured Pecos, "goes a man who's in a hurry about something."

He galloped his horse through Shadrock's dusty street until he turned the corner and reached the faded gate and unpainted porch where Grace Coleman had been waiting for these past ten days. He rolled out of the saddle and took off his hat as she came to the gate to meet him.

"I forgot," he grinned, "to—"

"—get me," she finished for him. "I'll be right with you."

Curtis Bishop was born in Tennessee but lived most of his life in Texas, where he traveled with rodeos and worked for several daily newspapers as a feature writer. Much of his newspaper writing dealt with characters, landmarks, and institutions of the Old West. In 1943 he also began writing fiction for the magazine market, especially Fiction House magazines, including *Action Stories*, *North-West Romances*, and *Lariat Story Magazine*. During World War Two, Bishop served with the Latin-American and Pacific staffs of the Foreign Broadcast Intelligence Service. His first attempt at a novel was titled "Quit Texas—or Die!" in *Lariat Story Magazine* (3/46). Subsequently he expanded this story to a book-length novel titled *Sunset Rim*, published by Macmillan in 1946. "Bucko-Sixes—Wyoming Bound!", which appeared in *Lariat Story Magazine* (7/46), was expanded to form *By Way Of Wyoming*, also published in 1946 by Macmillan. These were followed by *Shadow Range* (Macmillan, 1947), an expansion of "Hides for the Hang-Tree Breed" in *Lariat Story Magazine* (11/46). Although Bishop continued to write for the magazine market for the rest of the decade, his next novel didn't appear until 1950 when E. P. Dutton published *High, Wide And Handsome* under the pseudonym Curt Brandon. The pseudonym was necessary because Macmillan claimed it owned all rights to the Curtis Bishop name for book publication. *Bugles Wake* by Curt Brandon followed, published by E. P. Dutton in 1952. *Rio Grande* under the byline Curtis Bishop was published in 1961 by Avalon Books, the last of his Western novels. Living in Austin, Texas for much of his life, where he was able to study many of the documents of early Texas on deposit at the University of Texas' Special Collections, Bishop's Western fiction is informed by a faithfulness to factual history and authentic backgrounds for his characters, while he also was able to invest his stories with action and a good deal of dramatic excitement.